**Dirt and chips of gravel
sprayed into Longarm's face...**

The spreading charge splattered the ground in front of him. One pellet sliced down his back from shoulder blade to waist until it struck his belt and ricochetted off somewhere.

Longarm fired again. It did not occur to him until a moment afterward that there was no need for him to shoot again. But by the time he realized that it was too late. A soft lead slug from his Colt had already ripped the gunman's throat out, and the man was on the ground face forward with his lifeblood spilling into the dirt, and his legs beating a rapid tattoo of death on the hard ground...

TABOR EVANS

LONGARM

AND THE RANCHER'S SHOWDOWN

A JOVE BOOK

LONGARM AND THE RANCHER'S SHOWDOWN

A Jove Book/published by arrangement with
the author

PRINTING HISTORY
Jove edition/April 1986

All rights reserved.

ISBN: 0-515-08514-6

Jove Books are published by The Berkley Publishing Group,
200 Madison Avenue, New York, N.Y. 10016. The words
"A JOVE BOOK" and the "J" with sunburst are trademarks
belonging to Jove Publications, Inc.

PRINTED IN THE UNITED STATES OF AMERICA

Chapter 1

Longarm ambled into the office with a smile on his tanned face and a warm glow of repletion in his belly. He had just finished a heavy lunch and felt completely satisfied. He was picking his teeth with a thumbnail and he belched once before he nodded a civil greeting to Henry, the fussy clerk who guarded the portals to U. S. Marshal William Vail's private office. Longarm hung his snuff-brown Stetson on the coat tree behind Henry's desk and managed to force another belch. The rude sound brought a frown of disapproval to Henry's prim lips, and Longarm grinned evilly behind the smaller man's back. He was contemplating what else he might do to pick on Henry when the clerk said over his shoulder, "The boss wants you."

Henry sounded altogether too satisfied for Longarm's peace of mind. "He isn't gonna send me out with the weekend coming on, is he?" Longarm had certain plans for this coming weekend that he would prefer not to have interrupted. He had been looking forward to spending this Friday afternoon serving warrants in town, boring duty but necessary. At least it allowed him the privilege of getting out of the confinement of the office while remaining agreeably close to Miss Angela Trobiano—and he planned to allow certain other events to occur after supper.

The clerk shrugged, but the smug look of him made Longarm certain that Henry knew more than he was telling. Playing guessing games with Henry would not get him anywhere, though, so Longarm put on his most agreeable expression and let himself into Billy Vail's office without waiting for Henry to announce him.

"Howdy," he said with determined cheerfulness as he flopped casually into one of the red-leather-covered chairs in front of Billy's desk. "Have you eaten at that new place around the corner yet, Billy? Fine food." He neglected to mention Miss Angela, who served the food, and who had more or less promised to step out with him this evening after she was done with her work at the restaurant.

The federal marshal for the Justice Department's Denver district grunted something and continued rooting through the paperwork that was scattered over the surface of his desk. For the moment he ignored Longarm. He shuffled through one stack and then another and finally gave in and yelled, "Henry!"

"Yes?" The clerk was at the door within seconds, almost as though he had been waiting there to be summoned.

"Damn it, Henry, where's the Bell file? I can't seem to find it." Vail was still bent over the untidy mess of papers. Light streaming in through the window behind his desk shone brightly from his pink, nearly hairless dome.

"Would that be Bell, Horace I., boss, or Bell, James T.?"

"You know good and well which one I need, Henry."

"Oh, yes. Bell, Horace I. I believe the file is in your bottom left drawer."

"What the hell would it be doing there?" Billy Vail sounded irritated and more than a little flustered. "For that matter, how the hell would you know it's there if it is, which it shouldn't be?"

Henry shrugged and disappeared from the doorway, going back to whatever it was he did at the well and truly ordered desk he ruled in the outer office.

Vail opened the indicated drawer and with a snort that

2

might have been either satisfaction or disgust pulled out the necessary file folder. "There, damn it." He stuffed the folder unopened into a briefcase, then swept all the other papers into a single mass which he dumped without ceremony into another desk drawer.

"I could come back later when you aren't so busy," Longarm suggested quietly as he pulled a cheroot from his coat pocket and nipped the tip from it with his teeth. He reached for a match and spat the flake of twisted tobacco into his palm. This was no time to annoy the marshal by littering the rug.

"You sit where you are, damn it. I haven't time to go chasing after you a second time."

Longarm did not know when the alleged first time was supposed to have occurred, but he was not inclined to argue the point. He sat where he was.

Billy Vail made a quick final search of his now clean desk top, opened another drawer and took out a leather-bound writing case with pens and nibs and powdered ink, and put the final article into his briefcase, buckling it shut with another grunt. This one sounded a trifle more satisfied. He tugged down the bottom of his vest and began to put on his suitcoat and narrow-brimmed stockman's hat.

"Long," he said briskly, "you're in charge here."

"But—"

"None of that, now. I don't have time for it. My train leaves in forty-five minutes, and I still have to go home and get my suitcase."

"But—"

"Telegraphed request. Urgent. From the U. S. Attorney at Leavenworth. Damn good thing he messaged me, too, because those idiots at the prison wouldn't have. Seems this Bell fellow— Do you remember him? Never mind. Anyway, it seems the fools at the prison are intending to spring him on some technicality or other unless I get over there and clarify it. He's to be released at noon tomorrow, so I can't miss this train. I have to be there when they open the gates in the morning or we'll lose the bastard. So you are in charge of the office until I get back, which should be for the start of business hours Monday. All right? Good." Billy Vail had his hat on his head and his briefcase in his hand, and was already headed for the door.

"But, damn it, Billy, I—"

"No time for that, Long. You're the chief deputy, right? Right. You're in charge. See you Monday." Billy was at the door now and halfway through it.

He stopped and whirled around to face Longarm, the finger of one hand aimed straight at his chief deputy's startled face. "And mind, damn it. This isn't some schoolyard where you can play games and run in circles. While you are sitting at my desk, Deputy Long, you represent both the United States government and me. If you manage to screw up a simple Friday afternoon and Saturday morning of business hours, the government may forgive you, but I sure as hell won't. By the book, Long. Just do things by the book until I get back, and everything will be all right."

Billy Vail turned and hurried out of sight.

Longarm discovered that he had been holding his breath for the last minute or so. Now that Marshal Vail was gone and Deputy Custis Long was in charge the office seemed quiet and extraordinarily empty.

Longarm exhaled in a long, low whistle and turned to Billy Vail's desk, which seemed to be his desk, temporarily at least.

He sauntered to it, whistling openly now, and removed his brown tweed coat. He tossed the coat onto a peg on Billy Vail's private and personal coat rack, then eased down into Billy Vail's soft and comfortably padded swivel chair,

4

wiggling his butt into the best possible posture.

Grinning, he propped his stovepipe boots onto the edge of Billy Vail's desk and laced his fingers behind his neck. His cheroot, still unlighted, stuck out of the corner of his mouth at a jaunty angle.

"Henry!" he bellowed.

The clerk peeped around the edge of the door. "Yes?"

"I believe I should like some coffee now, Henry," Longarm said with a grin.

The grin faded. "And then I wish you'd tell me what in *hell* I'm supposed to be doing here."

Henry laughed. "I can do that," he said. He hesitated for a moment and added, "Boss." The way he said it was not entirely respectful.

Longarm looked around on the top of Billy Vail's desk for something to throw, but everything had been swept willy-nilly into a drawer and there was nothing handy. By the time Longarm fumbled the top drawer open and got a gum eraser poised to throw, Henry had disappeared.

Acting Marshal Custis Long—at least Longarm assumed the title went with the chore, although Billy had not exactly said so—handed Deputy Smiley a sheaf of subpoenas to be served, then settled back in Billy Vail's comfortable chair and resumed his former position, his boot heels resting on the unblemished edge of the broad, highly polished desk.

Smiley, a tall, lanky breed with dark eyes and a nearly critical need of a visit to a barber, stared at the offending boots for a moment before he turned to go. Longarm was not positive, but he thought he could see a faint tightening of the man's thin lips into something that might almost have been an expression of amusement.

Incredible. Despite the man's sunny name, Longarm could never recall having seen the dour deputy smile. *Naw,* he

5

thought as Smiley stalked out of the office. *Couldn't have been*. Longarm stifled a yawn and paid attention as Henry's bespectacled head appeared once more in the doorway.

"What is it this time, Henry? Is Guilfoyle back yet?"

"No, I expect he'll be tied up in court all afternoon and possibly through the weekend as well. You know how those lawyers can natter on."

Longarm grimaced and nodded. He knew all too well how a bunch of city-boy lawyers could tie knots in a good man's tail. There were times when Longarm thought it a hell of a pity that a bunch of damned lawyers were allowed to mess in the business of the law. Poor Guilfoyle could be tied up in court for weeks, sitting on the hardwood benches outside the damned courtroom until he got boils on his butt, just in case some lawyer with whiskers a cat could lick off might want to ask him another question. Longarm had been in that exact situation all too often himself in the past. He sympathized with the unfortunate deputy who was tied up in the boring ordeal of a trial that should have taken five minutes but would likely drag out for half of forever instead.

"So what's up?" Longarm asked. He had been in charge of the Denver district marshal's office for all of forty-five minutes, and he was already tired of it. And he had all the rest of today and half of Saturday to go before the office could be closed until the start of normal business hours on Monday morning.

"There is a young lady to see you, Longarm," Henry said.

Longarm's interest perked up. "Yeah?" His boots came down off the top of Billy's desk, and he sat up straight in the chair, his hands fluttering quickly to make sure his tie was not crooked and that his vest had not ridden up onto his belly. "Show her in."

He wondered fleetingly if the visit was being paid by

Miss Angela Trobiano. Their date for the night had, after all, only been hinted at. The very attractive young lady might be able to speak more freely away from her family's restaurant. He grinned.

But instead of the dark-haired and buxom Miss Trobiano, it was a complete stranger who showed up at the door. This young lady was pretty enough. Her blond hair was done up in a simple bun. She had delicate features, gray eyes, and a slender frame but with a nice hint of bosom and hip beneath a slightly stained and obviously faded dress that showed the wrinkles of long storage.

Longarm stood and motioned her toward the chair he had recently occupied in front of Billy Vail's desk. As he did so he made a further assessment of the girl.

She was, he realized as he looked more closely at her, still very much a girl, not yet a woman grown. Her dress and the outdated handbag she carried gave her an older appearance, but on close inspection he decided she probably was not much more than sixteen or seventeen. Lines radiating from the corners of her mouth and around her eyes he had taken at first for lines of maturity. Now he guessed that they were there because of worry, not years. Something was damn sure bothering her.

She moved stiffly to the indicated chair, looking almost brittle in motion, as if she were keeping a tight rein on herself for some reason she had yet to explain.

Her shoes, peeping from beneath the hem of her dress when she walked, were scuffed and worn and much too heavy for the town appearance she was trying to present. A country girl, he guessed, dressed in her seldom-used best and extremely nervous about this visit.

She coughed into her hand and turned her head away, a touch of color reaching her pale cheeks.

Damn, but she was pretty, Longarm thought.

He put that sort of thinking out of mind, or tried to, and reminded himself sternly that he was now representing the United States government in an official capacity and had no business thinking such thoughts during office hours.

Longarm did his best to assume a sympathetic elder-statesman expression as he asked, "What is it I can do for you, miss?"

"What? Oh." She blushed slightly and dropped her eyes toward her lap, where her hands, ungloved, were nervously picking at each other. "I'm...uh...Carrie Smith." She seemed at a loss for a moment. Her gaze flicked up toward the front of the desk, briefly surveyed the nameplate that rested there, and returned to her lap. "You are Mr. Vail, then."

Longarm shook his head, realized she could not see the gesture, and said, "No, miss. I'm just the marshal's chief deputy. My name is Custis Long."

That routine bit of information was enough to cause the girl's face to twist. She dropped her head into her hands and began unaccountably to weep, tears rolling out of her gray eyes and her shoulders sagging and shuddering from her sobs.

"I could be wrong," Longarm said gently, "but I believe that's the first time anybody's got *that* upset when I told them who I was."

The girl began to cry all the harder, but at least she did look up and pay a little attention to him. "I'm so...so... sorry," she said between sobs. "Truly, I am. But T-T-Tom is going to *die*, Mister Long. They're going to *hang* him. M-M-Monday morning. And I don't know what else to *do*. And you aren't even the marshal. And now I...I...." She broke down completely and buried her face in her hands again.

8

Longarm felt utterly helpless. He went around the desk to her side and knelt there. He thought she needed the physical comfort of a sheltering arm around her shoulders, but that would not have been seemly. So he did the next best thing, and patted her shoulder lightly until the crying subsided a little.

"Tell me about it," he suggested gently. "I'm not the marshal, but maybe I can help."

"B-but . . ."

"Take your time. Calm down a minute, and then tell me what this is all about."

"I'll try."

He continued to pat her shoulder, and she continued to cry, but after a few minutes the sobs became fewer and her shaking settled into a slow rocking back and forth, and after a time she was able to speak almost coherently.

The story she told was a simple one to a deputy U. S. marshal but a devastating one to a country girl from a hard-scrabble ranch out on the empty grass.

The Tom who was about to die was her older brother, Tom Smith. Thomas W. Smith, Jr., actually, named for her father, who had died not quite a year ago. Her mother was dead too, had died of an epizootic back in Ohio a while before her dad uprooted the family and moved them west to take up free land on the plains northeast of Denver.

The Smith family had tried to dry-farm the thin, virtually waterless topsoil, then quickly realized that the land was not suited to Ohio farming methods and converted to trying to raise livestock instead. Their only real asset on the free homestead land was a steady waterhole the elder Thomas Smith had developed along the course of a mostly dry stream bed.

Longarm suffered through the extraneous details of her

9

tale, even though it was one he had heard many, many times before. She would have to tell it in her own way or likely break down again.

After their dad died, the two young Smiths had no one else to go to and no place else to be. They stayed on, trying to run the place the way they thought their father would have. They were not doing particularly well, but they had not starved out yet, either. That was something, wasn't it?

Longarm agreed that that was a great deal indeed.

But now Tom was going to die, Carrie Smith wailed, and began to cry again. Now they were going to *hang* him. And all over something as silly as a horse.

They said he had stolen three horses from their neighbor, and now they were going to hang him. Just for that. Which wasn't fair, even if he had stolen the damned horses. She looked shocked with herself for having said a bad word like that, but stuck her chin out and made no apology about it. But, of course, he had *not* stolen any horses. So it *really* wasn't fair. Was it?

"I couldn't rightly say what's fair or what isn't, Carrie, without I know more about the case," Longarm told her gently.

"But that's why I came here, you see. To see the marshal. Because surely it can't be right or fair to hang a boy—he isn't a man, you know, though he tried to act like one— but it can't be right or fair to hang someone just for taking some silly horses that couldn't be worth more'n ten or fifteen dollars apiece. Even if he done it, which I *know* he didn't because he told me so."

Longarm sighed and patted her shoulder again. "Let me try to explain," he said. "It isn't what a horse is worth that makes the law the way it is. Why, a man could be caught red-handed stealing a prize bull worth a thousand dollars, and he wouldn't hang for it. He'd go to jail, sure, but he

10

wouldn't hang for it, because what he'd be taking would just be property. He'd be depriving the owner of something of value, and so he would go to jail, but he wouldn't hang.

"But with a horse, Carrie, a man would be stealing something more than just the worth of the animal if it was sold. A man or a woman out here *depends* on a horse. Folks out on the empty grass or 'way back in the mountains, they can need a horse awful bad when they need one. It can be the difference between people living or dying. Why, if you came down sick, say, and your brother had to get you to a doctor or you'd die, he would have to have a horse to do it, wouldn't he?"

She looked at him, her eyes red and swollen, and reluctantly nodded.

"Of course he would. He'd have to be able to hitch it to a wagon or get in the saddle and ride for help. And if you was so bad sick that you might die without help and he went out to the barn and all your horses had been stolen, why, you could die because of the lack of a horse. Or he could if the situation was the other way around and he was bad hurt and you were the one that had to go for help.

"So the law, Carrie, isn't punishing the horse thief for the value of the animal that's stolen. It's trying to protect the lives and the safety of the people who that horse has been stolen from."

She began to cry again. "But he didn't *do* it," she wailed.

"Now that, you see, is something else again."

Carrie Smith broke down again, and it was a good five minutes before Longarm could get any further sense out of her.

She had come to the U. S. Marshal's office, not knowing anywhere else to turn, with the idea that surely the government would have to protect her brother from hanging for such a thing as horse theft. And now this tall deputy who worked for the government said that it was right and proper for horse thieves to be hanged. That news was more than she could bear.

"Tell me why you think your brother didn't steal those horses," Longarm suggested, more to distract her from her misery than for any other reason.

"He . . . he *told* me he didn't," she said. "An' besides, I was there with him that whole day, you see. He couldn't have gone off an' stole anything because I was with him all that day. We were cleaning out the pond that day an' trying to get the pen around it tight because our neighbor's damn cows—" she had said the word again but seemed less stricken by it this time—"are always trying to get in, and there isn't enough water for our stock an' his too, you see. So we were working there together that whole day, but they didn't believe me when I told them that in court. They said I was his sister an' so I'd lie for him to save him an' . . . I forget what word they used for it, but the damn lawyer, who's a friend of the neighbor that brought this on us, he had a word for it that made me out to be a liar even before I ever said a word, and so the jury didn't believe me when I told them, and . . ." She began to cry again.

Longarm waited her out patiently. He was really only trying to be kind to her. Horse theft, except the theft of government animals, was an offense punishable under state or local law. The U. S. Justice Department would have no jurisdiction or interest in the matter.

The girl quit crying after another few minutes. Her expression took on a firmer set, and for the first time since she had entered the office she showed a little of the spunk that had brought her here.

"That damn Foster better watch his step, Mr. Long. If Tom hangs because of his lies I don' care if they hang me

12

too. If Tom dies, I'll get that George Foster if it's the last thing I ever do."

Longarm's head snapped up at the sound of the name, and he began to pay close attention to her for the first time.

George Foster. Longarm knew that brass-bound son of a bitch. Knew him slightly and knew of him even more, and nothing he had ever heard about George Foster had ever been good. The man was a hothead and a big-mouth, and he was asshole from head to foot.

"Tell me more about this George Foster and what he claims your brother done," Longarm said softly.

Chapter 2

Longarm had Henry bring the distraught girl a drink of water to help her calm down. Then he sat back in Billy Vail's chair and wondered what, if anything, he ought to do.

It was clear that the United States government had no official interest in the case. It had been handled in Denver County court, where the presumed theft had taken place, although the stolen stock owned by George Foster had been recovered on the Smith place in nearby Weld County.

According to the girl and to the newspaper article Henry scouted up for Longarm, Tom Smith had been discovered in physical possession of three horses wearing the Diamond F brand of noted local rancher George Foster.

The theft of the horses had taken place sometime early the previous Sunday. The recovery had been made Sunday evening, and young Tom Smith, Jr. had gone on trial Wednesday morning. The verdict was rendered that afternoon in time for a brief mention of it to be in Thursday's newspapers.

Damned quick justice, Longarm thought, when an awful lot of criminals could spend months in jail waiting for trial before their sharp-penciled counsel finally allowed them to reach a courtroom.

And now Tom Smith was set to hang bright and early on Monday morning.

The whole thing was too quick for comfort, even without the girl's protestations of her brother's innocence.

That was an indicator of big-mouth George Foster's influence with the local law, Longarm reflected. The man might be a son of a bitch, but he was not a fool. He was willing to grease his path by keeping the local politicians happy with heavy contributions during their election campaigns.

The name of the prosecutor given in the newspaper was that of the district attorney's brightest and most able assistant.

The newspaper had not bothered to mention it but, according to Carrie Smith, young Tom had had to defend himself against the charges. The Smiths had been too poor to afford defense counsel and, she said, had not really been aware of the severity of the charges anyway. The two youngsters knew Tom was innocent and simply had refused to believe that he could be convicted of a crime he did not commit. They had become afraid entirely too late to do him any good.

Longarm wondered bitterly if the judge who presided over Tom's case had been among the political office-seekers who received George Foster's generous financial support. Longarm did not know the judge, and knew nothing about him, but it would have been unusual if the judge had not been helped in his campaign by Foster's money.

Tom's side of the story, also unmentioned by the news article, was that he had been approached by three men he had never seen before. The three were riding three tired horses. They said they were in a hurry and wanted to swap horses with him, exchanging their tired mounts for three of the nags in the Smith corral.

Tom had thought the trade a good deal for the Smiths. Their own four horses were all heavy-bodied cobs better suited to pulling a wagon than to the riding that had to be done on the place now that they were out of dry land farming and into the raising of livestock. The three mounts the men wanted to swap were much better animals, and a little sweat was not going to hurt them. Given a few days to rest, they would be in fine shape again.

So Tom had made the trade and turned the new horses, which turned out to be George Foster's horses, into the corral. Then he went back to his work.

"I saw them myself, Mr. Long," the girl said. "I told the court that, but they didn't believe me."

Longarm nodded. "Could you describe them if I asked you to? I don't want you to right now, but could you if I asked?"

"Oh, yes. I did for the court too, but I don't think they were listening."

"Go on."

"I told them about the saddles too, but they weren't paying any attention then either," she said.

"Saddles? What about the saddles?"

"Mr. Foster, when he first came with the deputy sheriff, he was all upset about his saddles being missing. In fact, he seemed a lot more upset about the saddles that were taken than he was about the horses. I guess because one of the saddles was supposed to be kind of valuable or something. Special somehow, but I don't know anything about saddles. But then when it came to trial it was only the horses that they talked about, and nothing at all was said about the saddles. I tried to bring that up. I said if Tom had stolen the horses, which he hadn't, he wouldn't have needed to take three saddles too. So if he had taken them, why weren't they found at our place too? Because of course those men who rode the horses to our house changed the saddles to our horses and rode off on them. That's why there were no saddles there. But that assistant district attorney man told the judge there was nothing in the charges about saddles and so what I was saying wasn't . . . uh . . . relevant. I think that's the word he used."

Longarm nodded. "And Tom didn't object to that?"

The girl looked like she was going to cry again. "I didn't know he could. I expect he didn't know it either."

Longarm sighed. Those kids hadn't known a thing about what went on in a court of law. And there young Tom was trying to act as his own defense in a capital case.

George Foster and his tame pals sure had known, though.

Longarm found it interesting that when the case came to trial only the horses had been mentioned in the indictment. Foster definitely wanted the kid hanged, or at the very least out of the way for a very long time, when those charges were presented.

"Is there any reason why Foster would want your brother to hang?" Longarm asked.

"I . . . can't imagine why he would," Carrie said. "Although he has been trying to buy us out ever since Pa died. Maybe . . ." She looked frightened. Obviously it had not yet occurred to her, among all the other stresses of the past week, that there could be any motive beyond justice why Foster would want to press the extreme charges against her brother.

"You say he has been trying to buy your place?"

"Yes. I told you we were fixing the fence that day to keep his cows away from our little waterhole. Mr. Foster says we're robbing him of an awful lot of grass by fencing his cattle away from that water."

"Huh." Longarm scratched under his chin. The girl had said something earlier about keeping a neighbor's animals away, but at the time there had been no name mentioned.

Still, it could sure be the reason why Foster was being so hard with young Tom.

The way the homestead laws worked, a man could control

one hell of a lot of territory by filing ownership claims on a mere handful of acres, as long as those very few acres included all the water available.

A man who owned one watering spot here and another ten or even twenty miles away would in effect have tacit ownership of the whole stretch of grass between them if there was no other source of water for the herds that would be using all that grassland.

That would be motive enough for Foster to push the law to the limit against young Tom Smith. Motive enough too for him to neglect any side issues like missing saddles that might raise some doubts about the credibility of the charges against Tom.

The girl's story was beginning to look like an out-and-out railroad job, with her brother as the victim and George Foster as the big winner.

Longarm frowned and rubbed at the back of his neck. Damn it, though. Damn it! The case was tried and done with. Tom Smith, Jr. was set to hang. There was no federal angle to this thing at all.

There was no excuse in the world for Deputy U. S. Marshal Custis Long to be putting his nose into the matter.

Longarm looked at the girl. She was weeping again, very softly this time, making no sound. Only the movements of her thin shoulders betrayed her.

She was a pretty kid, and mighty vulnerable.

She had no place else to turn.

This was going to be a lousy weekend for her, sitting in some cheap room, likely, waiting for Monday morning to arrive. Waiting for her only brother to be led up the gallows steps to be hanged by the neck until he was dead.

Longarm felt sorry for her. He wished there was something—anything—he could do to help her, but he really could not.

He had no jurisdiction here. If he tried to butt his way into it he could get something worse than a wrist-slapping if the local people took offense.

Besides, he was in charge of the damned office until Billy got back, which would be Monday morning. By that time Tom Smith, Jr. would be dead.

Longarm scowled. If he took off and tried to do something to help the girl on his own, he would be as much as abandoning his post. Yet if he sat here and did his duty by the book, the way he was supposed to, Tom Smith, Jr. would die, and three horse thieves would get off scot-free.

It angered Longarm to see a thief go free, regardless of whether some other poor bastard had to pay for his crime. This way, with Tom Smith, Jr. hanging in the thieves' stead, it would be just that much worse.

The proper thing for Longarm to do, of course, would be to sympathize with the girl and try to soothe her feelings and send her around to somebody in the district attorney's office to see if she couldn't get a delay in the execution of sentence, like maybe on an appeal.

Longarm pulled his Ingersoll from his vest pocket and looked at the time. It was still early enough. She would be able to find someone in the office.

But, damn it, that was the very same office that had successfully prosecuted her brother just a few days ago. They were the ones who were responsible for the preparation of the gallows.

The few people Longarm knew over there were not so idealistic that they would be likely to buck the political pressures and raise a stink against a prosecutor in their own office and one of the county judges.

Longarm rubbed the back of his neck again. This kid was up the legendary creek, and her brother was fixing to die, and there was not a single damned thing Custis Long could do about it.

He had to do what he had to do, which was nothing— nothing at all.

All he could do was wish her well and send her out to wait for that gallows trap door to spring bright and early on Monday morning.

No choice about it, he told himself. It was none of his business. It was out of his hands.

Longarm carefully went over each and every option he had, and each time, every way he figured it, he came to that same conclusion. There was nothing he could do for her. Not without putting his own ass on the line.

He grinned. "Henry."

"Yeah?"

Longarm was already reaching for his coat by the time Henry stuck his head in the room.

"You're in charge here until I get back, Henry."

"But—"

"No idea when that will be, Henry. Maybe not till Monday morning."

"But the boss said—"

"I know that, Henry. He put me in charge. And now I'm delegating that to you. Right?"

"But—"

Longarm took the girl's elbow and pulled her to her feet. "C'mon, Carrie. We have a lot to do and no time to do it in."

Longarm dragged the confused girl out of the office, past an uncomprehending Henry, who almost certainly would be concluding by now that Deputy Custis Long was taking the weekend off to play private games with this distraught and tear-streaked girl.

21

To hell with it, Longarm decided. Henry could think what he damn well liked, and so could everyone else.

He was going to do what he *could* do. The hell with what he *had* to do.

Longarm walked beside the girl, having to shorten his stride to allow her to keep up with him without breaking into a trot. He was tall, well over six feet, with broad shoulders and narrow hips. He was a study in brown beside the small blond girl—brown hair, brown Stetson, drooping brown moustache, dark tan from sun and wind, brown tweed coat, broad corduroy trousers pegged into tall black boots. A Colt Model T. 44-40 rode at his waist to the left of his belt buckle, rigged for a cross-draw.

He slowed his normal pace for her benefit, but he did not mind that at the moment. He still was unsure of where he should be taking her.

There was so little time. The odds were very greatly in favor of failure now that he had been fool enough to commit himself to helping her. If he had had a few weeks, even one week . . . But Tom Smith, Jr. was going to die on Monday morning, unless Longarm was able to do something about that.

Longarm glanced down at the girl who walked at his side. He hoped to hell his judgment was not being affected by how very pretty and defenseless she seemed.

She was mighty vulnerable right now. He could see the fear stark and wide in those huge gray eyes.

It occurred to him—he could not help the thought, although he cursed himself soundly for it—that in her vulnerable, hopeful condition he could take her to his room and wrap his arms around her and comfort her, and her expression of hope and gratitude would be made in the only form she would have to offer.

22

The jut of her breasts was sharp and firm against the material of her old dress. The slight unconscious roll of her hips as she walked was provocative. He felt a strong stirring of desire.

Longarm cleared his throat nervously. In order to take his mind off the frightened girl and her slim, pliant body, he said, "Tell me more about your brother."

Her face, so small and so pretty, crumpled slightly, but she was able to hold back the tears with a swipe of her wrist over her eyes and under her nose. "I don't know what you want to know. He's all the family I have. He's fifteen, be sixteen this fall."

Longarm stopped abruptly, and the girl went on for another pace and a half before she realized and turned to face him. "Did I say something wrong?"

"Uh . . . no."

Carrie had said Tom was her *older* brother, and Tom was just fifteen.

"How old are you, Carrie?"

"Soon fourteen," she said. Her eyes were wide and innocent.

Longarm felt a quick heat rise to his cheeks after the things he had just been thinking about this child. He hoped there was no red in his cheeks that she could see, that the blush would be covered by the dark of his tan.

Soon fourteen. There he had been, a grown man who ought to know better, taking sideways looks at her, watching the wiggle in her walk. Thirteen years old, and he'd been thinking about snuggling up to her.

Men like you oughta have their balls cut off, Longarm told himself with disgust.

"Where are we going?" Carrie asked. Her tone was quite normal. Apparently she had not noticed anything unusual about him. Longarm was grateful for that small favor. He felt bad enough without having her guess what he'd been thinking.

"Your place," he said, not knowing himself until he heard his own voice say the words. "I'll want to start there, go down to Foster's from there, likely talk to the deputy who made the arrest. I'll just have to see what comes up. I wish I could tell you that I've got some fancy plan, but I don't."

"All right." She seemed to have confidence in him. The hope was stronger than the fear in her eyes now, although the fear was still there. It would remain there, never far from the surface, until Monday morning. Until there was no longer time for hope and there could be nothing left but the fear and the loneliness of being completely on her own in the world, without family or friends.

"How did you get here?" Longarm asked. He was assuming she had come in a wagon or possibly had gotten a ride to the rail line and came down that way.

"I borrowed a ride down with the deputy that brought Tom," she said. "The charges was here, but he was kept up home until time for the trial because that's where he was arrested."

Longarm nodded. "We'll want to rent a rig then," he said. "How long do you figure it?"

Carrie shrugged. "We haven't never been to Denver all that much. Be after dark, though, I should think. It's a ways out of town."

Longarm checked his watch again. There was so little time, and what there was of it seemed to be moving so rapidly. It was already mid-afternoon Friday. He wondered briefly about the exact time of execution ordered by the court but did not want to raise the question in her thoughts. Likely it would be dawn or just after.

There was a public livery a dozen blocks east. It was closer than going down to the Diamond K, where they knew him well enough to loan him an outfit if he asked for one. That would be cheaper, but it would involve the time to get all the way down there and the time it would take to cross the whole of Denver in order to head north again to the Smith place.

"We'll take a hack," Longarm said aloud, more to himself than to the girl. "We can rent a rig and be heading out in no time." Silently he reminded himself that this was not really official business. Better not to use a government voucher to pay the expenses. He would have to stand those himself for the time being. If he could figure an official angle on it later he could always turn it in on an expense account, although that would just be pointing a smoking gun at himself when Billy had to review the damn thing.

He turned and looked up and down the street. They were still right there on the federal building block, but there was not a hack anywhere in sight. *Never there when you want one,* he thought sourly.

The Smith place was not much. Longarm felt it was probably just as well that it was already dark, so he could not see the hopeless poverty of the little spread.

What little he could see by the light of the homemade tallow candles was about what he would have expected. Apparently the Smith kids could not afford to buy coal oil for the few lamps and lanterns around the place.

The house was a soddy, squares of plowed grass stacked like bricks to form thick walls that would be cool in summer and warm in winter, but annoyingly muddy when the rains came. Tom Smith, Sr. either had not known to or had not had time to plaster the outer walls with adobe mud and the children had not corrected their father's oversight, so the place would soon be in need of serious repair or replacement.

On the other hand, Longarm thought, if he was not able to help the children this weekend, there likely would not be need for anyone ever to worry about the soddy again. George Foster only wanted the waterhole.

"I'll fix you somethin' to eat quick as I get back, Mr. Long," Carrie said. "First I'd best go check on the stock and fetch back a bucket of water."

"Longarm," he corrected. "I thought we'd established that on the way up here."

The girl ducked her head in apology. "Yes, sir, Long-arm."

He smiled and shooed her into the soddy. "You go ahead and start the indoor things. I can bring the water."

"Are you—"

"I'm sure."

"Thanks. I left the gate open so's the stock could get in while I was gone. It's all right if you leave it open till morning. The pond is down there." She pointed vaguely into the night.

"I'll take care of it."

Longarm unhitched the rented horse from the light driving rig and got his McClellan saddle out of the back of the buggy. He had told the man at the livery that he needed a horse that could be driven or ridden, either one, and he hoped now that that was what he had. Carrie had already told him that their one remaining horse had been turned loose to fend for itself while she and Tom were down in Denver for the trial. They had had four but had traded three of them off, and of course no longer had the three they had received from those unknown visitors that day.

The livery horse accepted the saddle and Longarm's Spanish bit without protest. So far so good. He tied the horse to the post in front of the soddy and walked down the slight slope toward where Carrie had said he could find the pond her father had developed.

He found the waterhole all right, but there was no sign of any fence around it.

Leave the gate open, she had said. Hell, all he could find around the hole were some scraps of dried and twisted wood that might have been driftwood or might once have been a fence.

Longarm did a little fancy cursing under his breath. George Foster, no doubt, making sure his cattle were welcome at the water. Interesting that the son of a bitch had already gone to the trouble of taking Carrie Smith's fence down. Damned considerate of him to give her that help.

"Shit," Longarm said aloud as he went down to where the water should have been.

He knew damned good and well he was in the right place, because he could feel and hear the squish of his boots in mud. But there was damned little water standing in the hole.

She had said something this afternoon about there being just water enough for their own stock. Obviously she had been right.

Longarm was interested in getting a better look at this mudhole come daylight. He was curious about how big it had been as opposed to how small it was now. He was guessing, though, that Foster's beeves had been at the water for some time now, probably since before the trial began. If so, that sure told him that the bastard had been certain of the outcome of the court action.

Longarm slopped through the last few feet of mud until he finally reached some standing water. He filled the bucket Carrie had given him and lugged it back up toward the soddy.

The bucket was heavy enough to be a drag and a nuisance

for a grown man. Thinking of that little girl having to carry it—and then a bastard like George Foster going and making things all that much harder for the child—truly angered him. Longarm's temper was fairly hot by the time he got back to the soddy.

"I'll have some supper ready in a few minutes," Carrie said. She had a fire going already in the sheet-metal stove and was kneeling on the packed earth floor in front of it, feeding in hunks of dry cow chips.

Longarm took a quick look at the few scanty bundles on the shelves in the kitchen corner of the soddy. There was mighty little there for a person to eat, and he did not want to take food out of the child's mouth.

"Fix for yourself, Carrie," he said. "I don't want to take the time right now."

"But you have to eat something."

He smiled at her. "Don't worry about that. I'll get something at my next stop."

She stood and twisted her hands nervously into the apron that now covered her one good dress. She had told him on the drive up that the dress had been her mother's. "Will . . . will you be back tonight?"

"Do you want me to be?" Longarm had no idea if her nervousness came from the idea that there would be a strange man sharing the place with her through the night, or if she was afraid of staying here alone.

"Yes. Please," she said in a soft whisper.

"Then I'll come back quick as I can. When you get tired, Carrie, you go on and bar the door and go to sleep. I see you've a shed out by the corral. I can bed down there for the night. But don't fret. I'll be close by if you need anything."

She smiled, a very brief tugging at the corners of her lips, and Longarm realized that it was the first time he had

28

seen any kind of smile on her. It made her look even prettier. "Thank you," she said.

Without thinking about it, Longarm bent and gave her a light kiss on the forehead, the sort of quick, comforting peck she might have received from an uncle. The small display of affection unnerved her—probably she had not received any such since her father died—and for a moment she clung to him with a fierce strength, her breath and her tears hot on his skin through the layer of cloth that covered his chest.

"You'll be all right, Carrie. I'll do everything I can for you," Longarm told her.

"I...I know that." She was crying still, but she got control of herself and backed away from him.

"I'll be back later. Don't wait up for me."

She ran her knuckles under her nose and then into her eyes, sniffling as she did so. She nodded rather than answer in a voice that did not want to operate normally.

Longarm gave her another peck of reassurance on the forehead and went out to the rented horse. He had some miles to cover to reach the Foster spread, and damned little time in which to accomplish anything.

Chapter 3

George Foster's house was as grand as Carrie Smith's was poor. Longarm caught his unspoken assumption with a guilty start and corrected himself mentally. George Foster's house was as grand as *Tom* and Carrie Smith's was poor.

The Foster place was built of native stone, shaped and mortared and likely able to withstand centuries of summer heat and winter snow and year-round wind. A covered verandah ran the length of the front wall of the sturdy house. The light of dozens of oil lamps shone through the windows on both floors of the place. No one had to skimp on the pennies here. The house was lit up like a dance hall. Spread over the acres surrounding the house were corrals and sheds and outbuildings almost beyond counting.

Longarm sat on the small rise to the north of the headquarters and looked it over before he rode down.

Past the Foster place, some miles to the south, he could see a glow in the sky that would have been the bright lights of Denver in the evening. He had not realized until then just how near to the Foster ranch the booming city had come. The distance was probably not more than five miles, six at the very most. It was another eighteen or so back to the Smith place where Tom and Carrie's father had homesteaded. Just about the distance, he reflected, that a hard-pressed horse could make it at a ring-tail run.

Interesting, Longarm thought. Now that he was at the Foster place he did not have to be in all that great a hurry

31

to announce himself. He wanted a few minutes to do some thinking before he waltzed in there. He hooked a knee over the pommel of the McClellan and reached into his pocket for a cheroot.

As he lighted the cigar and drew the smoke deep into his lungs he thought about the things Carrie had told him during the afternoon.

Foster had first been carping about the loss of a saddle. Three saddles, actually, one of which had been valuable to him.

Three horses stolen and three saddles. And presumably no other tired exchange mounts left behind by the three riders when they picked up the Foster horses. Although Longarm would not put it past a prick like Foster to "neglect" to mention certain nonessential details of any given matter.

So whoever those three men had been—assuming that Carrie Smith was indeed telling the truth about all this— they had come to the Foster place afoot, helped themselves to horses and tack from the Foster sheds and corrals, and rode hell-for-leather on until the first relay of horseflesh gave out in the vicinity of the Smith place.

Which implied, of course, that they were headed some- where beyond the Smith place, traveling on a line roughly from Denver through Foster's land and past Smith's.

Who were they? Where were they going? And why were they in such a lather to get there?

Those were just a few of the things Longarm needed to figure out.

There were, of course, a hell of a lot more too. And no time for any of it.

He swung his leg back down from the pommel and shoved his boot into the stirrup. "C'mon, horse," he said in a low voice. The rented animal's ears waggled, and the horse began to pick its way slowly down toward the Foster headquarters. Longarm did not hurry it. Under saddle the animal had proven to be a stumble-footed creature, and he did not have any time to spare on healing broken bones.

Instead of stopping at the brightly lighted big house, Longarm rode past it and reined the mount to a halt in front of a low single-story structure that could have been mistaken for an equipment shed except for the light streaming out through filthy windows.

Someone inside heard his arrival and the door swung open.

"Who's it?" The man's voice was loud and just short of belligerence. He was wearing drawers and boots and carried a Kennedy repeating carbine in his hands.

Longarm announced himself by name but not title. He was on shaky enough ground just being here. He did not have to compound the sin by swinging his badge at people.

"Light, then, an' come inside."

"Thanks." Longarm swung down from the horse and tied the animal to the rail in front of the bunkhouse. It was the only horse there. The hands who were inside were settled in for the night.

Longarm stepped into the long, well lighted room and took his hat off.

The bunkhouse was nearly empty. Three men were seated around a rickety table with a deck of cards in front of them, and there was an empty chair available for the man who still stood in the doorway. There were bunks enough, though, to sleep a crew of a dozen and a half, and all of the bunks were laid out and had blankets or bedrolls on them. The floor was as filthy as the windows, littered with cigar and cigarette butts and overfull spittoons. Hair ropes and hack-amores and ragged hats were ranged on pegs over the bunks. Foster obviously was running a full crew, but most of the men were away for the evening. Likely in Denver, Longarm thought, with the growing outskirts of the town so close.

The man who had greeted Longarm set his carbine aside and motioned for Longarm to join them at the table. He was giving the deputy some speculative glances.

"Something wrong?" Longarm asked.

"Nope." The man thought for a moment. "Custis Long, eh?"

Longarm nodded.

"I've heard the name before."

Longarm shrugged.

The cowhand who was sitting with his back to the bunkhouse door swung abruptly about in his chair, and for half a heartbeat Longarm thought he had blundered into a scrap by coming here.

Then he saw that the cowboy, young and freckled, was smiling. "Hell, Long, I know you," the young hand said. "I seen you at the Brown Palace one evenin'." He rolled his eyes and whistled. "Some filly you was with that night."

Longarm grinned back at him.

"Fella I was with works at the Diamond K. Which is kinda a coincidence, me workin' for the Diamond F an' all. This fella I was with pointed you out to me. Said you're hell on wheels with a sixgun."

"A man shouldn't believe everything he hears," Longarm said mildly.

"Said you was a deputy Newnited States marshal?"

Longarm nodded. He might not have intended to advertise the fact, but he was not going to lie about it.

"Said those boys down at the K know you pretty good."

Longarm nodded again.

"You ain't here wantin' one of us, are you?"

"No," Longarm said. "Passing by is all, and I thought I might scout up some supper." It was a fact that he was damn sure hungry. It was hours past his usual mealtime, and while

34

he could go as long as he had to between meals it was not something he would do by choice.

"Hell, we can walk over to the cookhouse an' see if Cookie hasn't thrown the scraps to the hogs then."

There probably was not a hog closer than the city limits of Denver.

"I'd be obliged."

"Surest thing then, Marshal. I'll walk with you," the young hand said. He laughed. "See if'n I cain't talk you into introducin' me to that lady's sister."

Longarm had absolutely no idea who the cowboy might have seen him with. Not that it made any difference.

The cowboy pulled his shirt on and led Longarm across the packed yard to another building.

The cookhouse was as long and as low as the bunkhouse, but showed fewer lights. The long, scrubbed tables inside it were deserted at this time of night, but a light showed in the window at the south end of the place where the cook lived. The cook was at home, relaxing for the evening now that his work was done, a nearly empty bottle at his elbow and a finger-smeared dime novel in his hands.

The cowboy performed brief introductions, and the cook grumbled and swore but laid out a hefty platter of cold beef and leftover biscuits, then went back to his reading.

"Mind if I join you?" the cowboy asked.

"Of course not." Longarm tucked into his food, and the cowboy, whose name Longarm did not know, built himself a biscuit and beef sandwich too.

"You'd be after some desperado types?" the cowboy asked.

Longarm shrugged. "Nothing exciting, really. Mostly it's like that, you know. Routine. Serving warrants and writs of subpoena. It isn't all the excitement folks think it is."

The youngster looked disappointed.

"I saw in the paper the other day that you boys had some

excitement of your own recently," Longarm said, helping himself to another slice of the cold beef.

The cowboy's interest rose again now that he had a fresh audience for the story. "You must mean the horse theft an' them voting to hang the Smith kid."

"Uh-huh. It made the papers the other day."

"Really? I missed that." Even if he could read, the kid probably did not buy one newspaper a year. "I oughta look that up an' cut it out to send to my ma back home."

"The Thursday papers," Longarm said. "The story wasn't much, though. How was it that it really happened? I mean, they didn't go into much detail."

The kid told him very much the same story that had been in the *Rocky Mountain News,* although with some embellishments.

Longarm heard him out, then frowned slightly. "Wasn't there something about some saddles too? I never got that part quite clear."

"Oh, yeah," the cowboy said negligently. "But that part all died down." He chuckled. "Mr. George, though, he was damn sure fit to be tied las' Sunday. He come out to saddle an' go off for a ride." The cowboy winked. "Never said where he was gonna ride to, if you know what I mean, but he was sure some kinda pissed when his purty saddle weren't there in the shed."

The cowboy's implication seemed clear enough. The boss man had himself a lady friend somewhere, although Longarm was quite sure that Foster was married. "Fancy saddle, was it?"

The hand whistled and rolled his eyes. "Fancy? I mean t' tell you it was. Went down to Pee-eblo and had him a real good 'un made by Frazier, and you know there's no finer than that."

Longarm nodded. The Pueblo saddlery was becoming

known wherever men used horses to work cattle, and the reputation was well deserved.

"And then," the cowboy went on, "he brought this brand new Frazier back up to Denver. Afore he ever put his butt in the seat he took it down to old Mr. Gunderssen and had a lot of cunning little German silver inlays put onto the skirts an' behind the cantle and like that. Come out awful pretty, it did, and Mr. George, he was real proud of it. Used it only for special, and that's why he was so pissed when it wasn't there Sunday morning."

Longarm chuckled. "Got himself his own Denver filly, does he?"

"Uh . . ." The cowboy looked around to make sure the cook was not in sight, but the man had long since retired to his own pursuits. "This is just between you an' me?"

"Sure. Hell, we're just talking, anyhow."

"Yeah. Well, Mr. George, he takes off every chance he gets an' rides up north a few miles to what used t' be one of the line camps, though now of course the Diamond F range is way the hell an' gone beyond this old camp. Anyhow, he's got it fixed up real nice, they tell me. Though I've never been the one as takes supplies there and the like." He rolled his eyes again. "The boys do say there's *some* fine reason for a man to make the trip. Whew!" He grinned, and Longarm grinned back at him. The cowboy seemed a horny sort of youngster who liked to envy other men's conquests without having much of his own experience to brag about. Longarm knew a fair number of men like that, although he never truly understood why they did not just go out and find their own source of supply.

"So anyway," Longarm said, bringing the conversation back toward its original point, "what about the boy that was convicted of stealing the horses? Did you know him?"

"Sure, we all of us knew him. Nice kid, too. And a

37

sister?" He whistled again. "She's a mite young, but damn if she ain't gonna be a looker when she gets another year or two on her." He laughed. "Would be now, for that matter." The cowboy winked. "My old daddy always told me that the way you see if they're big enough is to stand 'em in a barrel. If their head sticks out o' the barrel, they're big enough."

Longarm had heard the saying often enough before. He knew what was coming but remembered to snort politely when the cowboy came to the punchline.

"Know what you do if the head don't stick out? You cut the damn barrel down." The cowboy broke up laughing at his own wit.

Longarm smiled. "Maybe I should stop in there too if I get in the neighborhood."

"Yeah, that girl is likely lonesome with her brother gone." He leered happily for a moment, then sobered a bit. "Tell you what, though, Longarm. All crappin' around aside. That there kid they're fixing to hang, he was a gutty little pup. Won't ever live long enough to shave, I reckon, but that never stopped him from turning a man's day of hard work. I think if he'd been left alone, if he hadn't gone an' fucked up by stealing them horses, I mean, he'd have made a go of 'er over there."

"Really?"

"Yeah, but that's another opinion I ain't supposed to have around here. Them kids was a thorn in Mr. George's side, layin' right on the north side of the Diamond F range like they was."

"How's that?" Longarm asked, pretending to misunderstand. "I thought Foster had a world of good grass here."

"Huh! He *wishes* he did. His mistake was taking up a place so close t' the big city, you see. Thought it was a good idear at the time, I expect, since it was so close to where the railroad was gonna come. The idear was to have a jump on all the other shippers. Walk our cows down to the rails without hardly having to lose a pound of tallow an' be able to ship them fat. Better profit that way, you know."

Longarm nodded.

"What he didn't figure on was the damn city growing the way it's done. So now half the grass we used to use down to the south is all covered with houses an' salad gardens an' rowdy houses." The cowboy winked and said, "Which ain't all bad, mind you. But, hell, Longarm, there's gas lights and silk-pants women in a place *I* can remember using for a line camp. And I ain't been here all that long." He shook his head.

"So north is the best way Foster can go if he wants to expand?" Longarm asked.

The cowboy snorted. "Expand, hell. He's lost so much graze to the street developers an' the pig farmers and such that it's all we can do trying to hold 'er even."

Longarm shoved a final bite of beef and biscuit into his mouth and sat back, smoothing his moustache and reflecting. George Foster's cowhand had unknowingly provided Longarm with an ample motive for Foster to want swift and certain "justice" for Tom Smith, Jr.

But parts of the thing simply did not hold water. Those horses really had been taken from the Diamond F. Three saddles truly were missing from the place. Carrie Smith had genuinely seen three men come to make the exchange of horses with young Tom.

It was not really likely that Foster had been behind that. Not with his best fancy saddle being taken. Longarm could almost—but not quite—believe that Foster would fake a theft of some saddle stock and a few nondescript saddles just to put some pressure on young Smith.

But he could not believe that the man would deprive himself of his expensive courting saddle when he did it.

Besides, much as Longarm hated to admit it to himself, George Foster was a first-class bastard, loud-mouth and bully. But the man was not truly dishonest enough to fake the theft.

He was the kind who would push it to all the self-advantage he could get once it happened. But Longarm did not think even George Foster would deliberately stage a robbery and then have a boy hanged for it.

The man had come up years ago from Texas, driving a herd of mixed stockers over the Goodnight–Loving Trail by way of the terrible Horsehead Crossing of the Pecos. He was tough. Only the very tough survived that route, man or beast either one.

And George Foster had his share and someone else's of raw pride. The man would push and chisel and claw. But Longarm did not believe he would do anything that would make him seem dishonest *in his own eyes*.

That was the key to George Foster. The son of a bitch was too proud to do anything that would diminish him in his own opinion.

And deliberately setting up Tom Smith, Jr. for a hanging was not Foster's style.

So there was a hell of a lot that Longarm still needed to learn, and he was beginning to believe that the Diamond F headquarters was not the place to look for it.

Longarm pushed his empty plate away and took his Ingersoll from his vest. Precious hours had already passed, and all he really had from here was a description of the missing saddle and the information that Foster had himself a piece of fluff on the side.

Talking with Foster himself was not likely to get him anywhere at this point. With the trial over and done with,

Foster would have to stand by the story he had told under oath, however the truth might have been bent during that proceeding. The man's pride would demand it.

Maybe, though, Longarm thought, the girl friend could shed some light on what Foster's private feelings and beliefs had been.

The cowboy had said the old line camp was to the north, which was the direction Longarm had to travel from here anyway. It would be worth swinging by and asking.

He pulled out two cheroots and offered one to the cowboy, who eagerly accepted it. Longarm casually got directions to the former line camp as they walked back to Longarm's rented horse.

"Thanks for the grub," Longarm said as he mounted.

"My pleasure," the cowboy said. "You stop in here any old time." He grinned. "Next time I see you in town, Longarm, the treat's on me."

Longarm smiled at him, knowing good and well that by the time the story of this visit was told in the Denver bars, he and this cowhand whose name he did not even know would be old pals.

He waved and reined the horse around to the north, away from the brightly lighted mansion George Foster had built for himself and his wife.

Chapter 4

"Hello. You must be Randy." The voice was as sweet as cane syrup, the long spill of unbound hair reaching to her waist the color of honey.

"Uh, yeah." Longarm honestly misunderstood what she had said. He mistook the name for a description, randy as in horny rather than Randy as in Randolph.

She had come out of the small, stone-walled house as soon as he rode into the yard and stood now at his stirrup.

She walked the fingers of her right hand up the inside of his thigh, tantalizing and teasing. His response was immediate, and damned near painful in its urgency.

The woman smiled at him and invited him down. It took him no time at all to comply with the welcome.

"You can put your horse in the pen over there." She laughed gaily. "After all, dear, you shan't be needing it again until morning."

Longarm was dumbfounded. Did she greet everyone who rode in like this? Or had it just been too many days since old George had been able to get away for a visit?

Whatever the reason, well . . . he was now damned well as randy as she had suggested.

And with a woman like this one he was not likely to kick her out of bed. Not unless he thought there was more thrashing room on the floor.

Silk-pants women, that cowboy had called them. Well, this was one, in spades.

She was all curves and scented hollows, satin skin pink and rosy. Perfume wafted on the air that surrounded her. She had long hair, rouged cheeks and lips, nails long and brightly polished.

Oh, my, Longarm thought as he followed her into the former line camp.

Longarm had seen a hell of a lot of line camps in his time. They were crude affairs, mostly as attractive as a boar's nest and generally with much the same odor.

This place was a miniature mansion, the floor covered with soft Aubusson rugs and the furnishings elegant.

But the elegance of the single room could not begin to compete with the elegance of the occupant.

She was the kind of woman who could put drool onto the chins of strangers who passed on the public streets.

And in her own private place . . . and her wearing nothing but a filmy, sheer little robe sort of thing . . . well . . .

She walked, Longarm trailing dutifully behind, until she reached the side of the huge brass bed that dominated the place. Then she turned and held her arms out to him, her eyes half closed with desire, her head lolling loose atop that sleek, satin column of slim neck.

Longarm did the gentlemanly thing. He kissed her, and was startled by the low, sensuous moaning that issued from her throat as her tongue darted and danced within his mouth. Her breath was sweet, lightly flavored with mint.

"Mmmmmm. Lovely," she whispered.

She shrugged her shoulders, and the garment fell away, leaving her nude under his hands.

Her flesh was cool velvet. Her breasts were soft, rose-tipped mounds that filled his hands and then his mouth as he bent his head to savor the taste of her.

Her hands were busy, working with quick skill to help

him out of his clothing without ever once losing the contact between them.

Longarm was befuddled, but he had not lost his senses altogether. He grabbed his gunbelt before it could fall to the floor and draped it quickly over the brass bedpost, then let her do the rest of the job of getting rid of the annoying clothes that separated them by a scant fraction of an inch.

The woman finished undressing him and smiled. She licked her lips in apparent anticipation and drew him onto the broad, soft bed. "Oh, yes. So lovely." Her whisper was throaty, hoarse with desire.

He took no time for preliminaries. He let her guide him onto and into her, and she gasped as he filled her. There was a slight change in the quality of her smile now. It was softer, brighter, somehow more sincere.

"You don't have to wait for me, dear," she whispered as he moved slowly within her. She whispered into his ear and followed the sounds with her tongue probing that same ear. "Hurry, please."

Longarm speeded his strokes, filling her to capacity with every thrust. He could feel her body stiffen beneath him as his speed increased. Her hips began to bump and writhe in short, abrupt, spasmodic contractions as her pleasure built with his.

When he came, burying himself deep in her with a final lunge, she cried out and clutched him to her with arms and legs and greedy mouth.

Longarm lay where he was for several minutes, enjoying the warmth of her skin against his, pillowed on belly and breast. Then, with a sigh, he withdrew from her and rolled to the side. She rolled with him, pressing herself against him as if there could not be enough contact between her body and his.

45

She ran her hands over his chest and toyed lightly with his nipples, then lower, across his stomach to cup his balls in the palm of her hand. She sighed again.

Longarm felt like sighing himself as she twined her fingers in his pubic hair and teased his shaft.

Her eyes opened wide with surprise and joy as he began to stiffen again.

"Really?" she asked.

He grinned at her.

Her tongue began to follow the path her fingers had recently taken, starting at his nipples, circling them slowly, tasting the thin film of sweat on his skin. Finally, she drew him deep into her mouth, engulfing him with heat and desire.

She moaned low in her throat and held him there, her head not moving but the slow, steady suction she was applying threatening to drive him mad.

Longarm let her bring him close to the brink that way, but pulled her away before he could finish. She smiled and opened herself to him, and again he entered her.

It was quieter this time, slower. He ignored her thrusting, humping, teeth-grinding spasms and took his time, enjoying every scent and texture of her, until finally he could hold back no longer.

This time when he pulled away and lay at her side she stayed where she was, limp and exhausted. She did not stir again until Longarm rolled onto his side and reached down to the floor to fumble in his clothing for his cheroots and matches. She looked at him with a warm, quiet smile.

"Thank you," she whispered. "You are a very special visitor, Randy."

Longarm felt a shock of realization as the error corrected itself. He sat upright and tried very hard to keep himself from laughing.

Longarm sat in the overstuffed armchair with a cheroot in one hand and a glass of whiskey in the other. The whiskey was not rye, but it was decent.

Celia sat in the slightly smaller matching chair beside him. She was over her anger now. The kicking, snarling, pillow-throwing fury she had displayed when she too discovered the error had finally been replaced by laughter and, now, acceptance.

She looked at him out of the corner of her eye—an almost golden hazel, he had discovered—and a wing of fine honey hair swept down over the curve of her cheek to lie on her naked breast. She began to chuckle again. Longarm did too, and within seconds they were both laughing loud and hard at the mistake. Although it had taken him the devil's own time of fast talking to convince her that he really had misunderstood when she called him Randy.

The error could have been, should have been, disaster. But he could not now say that he was sorry it had happened.

Weak with laughter, her slightly rounded and incredibly soft belly still contracting with aftershock spasms of it, Celia Ames stood and bent to give Longarm a brief kiss on the lips, then went to refresh both their drinks.

She sighed when she returned to her chair and reached out her right hand languidly to hold his. "You really are a delight, Custis. I suppose there is no harm in admitting what you have already seen for yourself, dear, so I shall make the admission baldly. The truth is, dear, that I become so weary of pretending pleasures that I rarely feel." She smiled. "But with you, dear, no pretense is necessary. You give at least as much as you receive. And that is rarer than you may ever know."

Longarm squeezed her hand, then removed his fingers

from hers so he could take another drink. He began to laugh again.

Celia raised an eyebrow in his direction.

"I was just wondering," Longarm explained. "What happens if friend Randy shows up now?"

"Oh, dear. That would be quite embarrassing."

"Should I leave?"

She shook her head quickly. "Don't. Please."

"And if Randy shows up?"

"I shall think of something, dear." She laughed. "I always do."

Celia was a kept woman and admitted it. She was a plaything for George Foster and quite obviously a favor he was prepared to bestow on his friends as well. But damned if Longarm didn't like the woman anyway. There was a basic honesty about her that went beyond her physical beauty—which was undeniable itself—that made her all the more attractive.

Even now, thoroughly spent after their recent exertions, the sight of her, naked and at ease beside him, brought a fluttering stir of fresh desire into his gut.

Celia saw the beginnings of that desire. She laughed out loud with pleasure at the sight and slid out of the chair to her knees. She came to him like that, kneeling in front of his chair, and laid her warm, soft cheek on his thigh.

She poised herself over him, lips parted, her breath warm, and let his growing erection rise to meet and then to enter her.

The last thing Longarm saw before he closed his eyes and put his head against the back of the chair, giving himself over to the sensations she was treating him to, was Celia's smile.

Later, he thought. There was time enough now. Later they could talk.

· · ·

Longarm was dog tired by the time he returned to the squalor of the Smith homestead. He would have liked to have stopped miles back and bedded down under the stars, but a promise had been made. He told Carrie he would be back.

He dismounted, stripped his saddle from the horse, and turned the animal into the small pen near the soddy. He raised his head and looked up toward the distant stars wheeling slowly through the clear night sky. Past one o'clock, he judged. Closer to two. No wonder he felt so damned tired.

He was heading wearily toward the shed and his bed for the night when he heard the creak of a door swinging on unoiled hinges. A moment later Carrie came out into the night air to join him. She wore a long gown of some age-worn material, and she was barefoot.

"Good evening," Longarm said with a tip of his hat toward the child. "I didn't mean to wake you."

"You didn't," she said. "I was awake. I . . . couldn't sleep until I knew you were back."

He was doubly glad now that he had taken the trouble to return before he bedded.

She shivered and wrapped thin arms around her narrow body. "Would you do me a favor?" she asked.

"Sure."

"Would you . . . come inside for a little? If you wouldn't mind. I'd . . . feel better if you sit with me, just for a few minutes, and maybe talk?" She was hesitant, as if the favor would be much too much for him to grant.

She was still a child, Longarm reminded himself. She was alone, and she was frightened, and likely every time she closed her eyes and tried to sleep she would be seeing only the sight of her brother, her only kin, hanging from a gallows.

"Sure." He smiled. "Besides, I wanted to talk with you anyway. I need to get a description of those men who stopped here to trade the horses. I forgot to ask you about that before, and I have to know. Okay?"

She nodded, obviously grateful for the company, and led the way inside the tiny soddy. The contrast between this tattered homestead and the opulence of George Foster's hideaway was extreme.

Carrie lit a candle and set it on the table. "Would you like me to make you some coffee? We have a lot left. Pa used to drink it all the time, but neither Tom or me cares much about it."

"No, thanks. It'd just keep me awake. If you wouldn't mind, though, I'd like to bring a bottle in and have a drink while we talk."

"Oh, I wouldn't mind. Anything you want to do, Mr. Long. Anything at all," she said quickly.

He went out to the shed where he had left his saddlebags and returned with his traveling bottle of good Maryland rye. The drink went down warm and smooth, spreading its heat quickly through his belly and taking the rough edges off his need for rest.

"Could I try some of that?" Carrie asked.

Longarm shook his head. "Too young."

"I am *not*." She sounded indignant. "I'm a woman grown." Longarm gave her a questioning look, and she blushed. "Well, practically."

He smiled at her and said, "You will be soon enough, Carrie. No need to push it. Besides, ladies don't care for hard liquor."

She sighed. "I'll never be a lady nohow, Mr. Long. If . . . if they do that to Tom, we both know how I'll end up. It won't be as no lady, neither."

Longarm looked into her eyes. So very young, still so

50

very innocent. Yet the body that was beneath the flimsy, much-worn flannel of her nightshift was already quite undeniably appealing. The cowboy back at the Diamond F had noticed. Longarm could not help but see either. The material of the nightshift was worn so thin that he could see the dark rosettes of the child's nipples where they pressed against the cloth. Her breasts were sharp-tipped and firm, with that rising tilt and tenderness that only youth can achieve.

She would be a hit on the line.

For a very little while.

A few months, a year at the most. Then her skin, so fresh now, would be coarsened and gray from the constant touch of strange men with whiskey on their breath and likely as well with diseases infesting their bodies.

A very little while of that and the child would lose her freshness. Her body would thicken, her speech become as coarse as the texture of her flesh.

The diseases and the abuses would claim her, and by the time of her fifteenth birthday she would be just another whore, working the line, spreading herself open to strangers in exchange for pennies.

Longarm shuddered. Carrie had already resigned herself to this fate. His stomach churned with disgust as he thought of what would surely happen to her. Unless he was able to do something, any damn thing, to stop her brother from hanging.

He even thought fleetingly about a wire. He could ride north to the nearest town with a telegraph office and send a wire to the Denver County authorities.

But on what grounds? On whose authority?

Without authority, without justifiable grounds, there would be no stopping it.

Longarm pulled the Ingersoll from his vest pocket, realizing as he did so that he had probably looked at the watch more today than he had on any three days since he had come to own the instrument, and once again checked the time. There was so terribly little of it, and what there was was as fleeting as quicksilver.

He took another drink from his bottle and stood.

"Mr. Long."

"Yes, Carrie?"

"I'm no so awful young, you know. And I truly would do anything to help Tom." She arched her back, deliberately thrusting the twin spears of her young breasts against the cloth that covered her.

Longarm smiled and bent to give her a chaste kiss on the forehead. "You don't have to prove anything to me, Carrie. I'll do everything I possibly can to help you and Tom. I thought you knew that already."

"Oh, I do. Truly I do. But..."

He patted her shoulder. "Good night, Carrie. I'll probably be gone before you wake in the morning, so don't worry about it. And I'll be back just as soon as I can. That's a promise."

"All right." She sounded subdued but, he thought, relieved as well.

"Good night," he said again. He picked up his bottle of Maryland rye and went out to the chilly solitude of the harness shed.

He was more weary now than he could remember being in a very long time. And he knew full well that it came not from simply being tired. Physical exhaustion was something he had long since learned to accept.

The thing that was wearing on him now, dragging at the very marrow of his bones, was the weight of responsibility that he carried.

For Tom Smith, Jr., who might well die on Monday morning.

For Carrie Smith, whose childhood would turn into a living nightmare if he failed.

He shivered. He did not dare fail. He could not allow that to happen.

But there was so damned little time.

He closed his eyes and dropped into a fitful, restless sleep, hating the necessity for that delay even while he acknowledged it.

Chapter 5

Longarm was saddled and gone well before dawn. He had slept only a few hours, and it was not enough, but it would just have to do. He had wakened as fretful as when he went to sleep, nervously conscious of the passage of time while he lay in his blankets, and no amount of mental persuasion had been able to convince him that he should go back to sleep. So he saddled the horse and rode out of the Smith yard in the chill air that precedes the first warmth of the morning sun.

He had only the vaguest idea of where he was going. Before he lined the rented horse out for the trail he sat on the far bank of the dry creek where Tom Smith, Sr. had developed his water supply and did some figuring in his head.

Back that way was Denver. Back there would be the Diamond F. Here was the Smith place.

He tried to draw an imaginary line from one through the next, to this point and then beyond in a reasonably straight course.

That was the direction the three men would have been taking when they fled Denver, stopped at the Diamond F to steal horses and saddles, and then made the fatal exchange here at the Smith place.

Fled?

It had come to his mind without conscious deduction.

Yet it was the only logical reason for the men to act the way they had. They had been fleeing from something or from someone. They had to have been.

Out of Denver on foot for the five or so miles that separated the outskirts of the city from Foster's headquarters. On foot as far and as fast as was reasonably possible. Sneak into the corrals and the sheds that surrounded the Diamond F headquarters like so many weeds.

Steal the horses and fog it like hell in *this* direction, stopping only to swap horses with Tom Smith, Jr.

Or had they?

That was something that had not occurred to Longarm until now. He and presumably everyone else was assuming that the thieves had made the single relay exchange of horses, because only the one exchange was known.

It could well be, though, that there had been another relay somewhere up the line, perhaps even several swaps. If they were in that kind of hurry there was no telling how far they wanted to run.

No one would have learned of the second exchange, because Tom Smith, Jr. was not out looking for stolen horses. As far as he knew at the time, the whole thing had been a fair and legal trade. He had broadcast no word for anyone to watch for the three horses that had been ridden away from the Smith place. It was entirely possible that the same thing would have occurred at all of the places trades would have been made once the first three horses were stolen.

Longarm groaned aloud to himself, and the horse flicked its ears in silent response.

Lordy, he thought. In a week's time those three men could have traveled clear to Canada if they were making swaps every fifteen or twenty miles and pushing their horses hard.

They could already be beyond a deputy U. S. marshal's

jurisdiction—never mind that he *had* no official jurisdiction in this matter to begin with—and, if that were so, Tom Smith, Jr. was as good as dead already.

He shook his head and bumped the horse into a lope as the first pale hint of the coming dawn gave him a bit more light to see by.

He felt like he was being pursued. The only thing wrong with that was that it was time that was chasing him, and he had no weapons to defend against the turning of the clock.

It was smoke that drew him to the isolated cabin. Smoke and the very welcome thought of breakfast bacon sizzling over the morning fire. All he carried in his saddlebags at the moment was a meager handful of dust-dry jerky. He had meant to restock his traveling supplies the last time he came in but had not yet gotten around to it. He had had no time for such details before he left Denver with Carrie.

Now that he could see the smoke that would almost surely guide him to his breakfast the hunger was knotting and gnarling in his belly, and saliva flooded his mouth at the thought of food.

He angled the horse away from the path he had been following and rode toward the column of dark smoke that hung on the still air. Another hour or less and the wind would have picked up, and he might not have seen the smoke. He was already grateful to whoever it was who was cooking.

He topped the last rise and his jaw muscles drew tight. The smoke came not from a breakfast fire but from the smouldering roof of a soddy built very much like Tom Smith's soddy.

The disrepair back at the Smith place, however, came from the passage of time. Here the sod-covered pole roof sagged as the result of fire.

And the fire had been no accident. Longarm was sure of that.

The peeled poles of the corral gate had been thrown down in the dust of the yard, and the corral was empty.

The wooden door of the soddy sagged drunkenly, the top hinge shattered and the bottom bending under the full weight of the partially open door. A wagon with one wheel broken, the spokes smashed by blows from something hard and heavy, sat outside the door of the soddy.

There was, incredibly, the wooden, unpainted shaft of an arrow protruding from the side of the wagon box.

Indians? A hostile Indian attack *here?*

Longarm was having difficulty believing that even before he rode slowly down into the yard with his Winchester in one hand and the reins in the other.

There had not been hostilities this close to Denver in a dozen years or more. Things were even calm at the moment up north on the reservation lands. If any of the tribes had been making a breakout, the marshal's office would have been informed of the danger. And Longarm had been away from the office only a matter of hours.

He rode cautiously, though. There is a wide gap between incredulity and damn-foolery. He was willing to engage in the one but he sure as hell intended to avoid the other. The Winchester was held with the butt on his right thigh, the hammer drawn back and a cartridge in the chamber. If anything moved...

The horse was nervous. It skittered and sidestepped, reluctant to move closer to the soddy. Its nostrils flared, and Longarm figured it was smelling something that still escaped his own keen sense of smell.

The animal might have been tested under gunfire half a hundred times and stood as solid as rock, but if so Longarm did not know it. The animal was an unknown quantity to him in that way, so as soon as it began to worry at the bridle he halted it and stepped out of the saddle.

Keeping an eye on the soddy and as much as he could see around it, he wrapped the reins around the top corral rail and left the horse while he moved cat-footed and silent toward the house.

He reached the wagon first and swiftly dislodged the arrow shaft from the plank side of the box.

He snorted out loud when he saw the pathetic attempt some fool had made to blame this on Indians.

The shaft of the arrow was dry and cracked with age. The fletching was no more than a twist of songbird feathers tied at the base of the shaft with a piece of ancient gut. The head, which had not been driven deeply into the wood, was a bird point chipped painstakingly out of shell.

The damned arrow had to be as old as Longarm or older. And even if it had been new and serviceable, it was made by the Caddo tribe. The Caddos now were as good as extinct and had lived twelve, fourteen hundred miles from Denver, way the hell and gone down toward the Gulf in East Texas.

Whoever had tried to misplace the blame for this one had done a poor job of it. Longarm laid the relic in the wagon—someone must have valued the thing or it would not have been preserved so carefully for so long—and moved in on the soddy.

The sharp stench of smoke was strong here. But there was another smell too now that he was close. The new odor was copper-sweet and ugly. It was of blood freshly spilled.

Longarm paused outside the broken door of the soddy. He uncocked the Winchester, leaned it against the front wall of the house, and palmed his Colt instead. If there was danger inside the fight would be at close quarters now, and the revolver would be quicker than a rifle.

He considered for a moment. The book said that the

proper procedure for entering a room where felons might be was first to announce oneself as a peace officer and then make the entry. That was what the book said.

On the other hand, books do not get gutshot when some son of a bitch has been warned and comes up with a sawed-off scattergun instead of a plea for mercy. Real life only rarely follows someone else's book.

Longarm held the Colt ready, tensed his muscles, and flung himself through the door in a swift rush. He ended up sprawled in the dirt of the floor with no target for the searching muzzle of the .44.

That was just fine by him. He would rather enter a hundred places with misplaced prudence and pay a hundred useless cleaning bills than to take a chance just once and get his head blown off.

There were no targets in the smoky interior of the house, but the place was not empty, although Longarm wished it had been.

The first figures he saw were those of children. They were lying like a pair of discarded rag dolls on the quilt that covered a homemade bed in the near corner of the house. There was nothing he or anyone else short of a preacher could ever do for them again.

A faint rasping sound in the far corner of the place brought the muzzle of the Colt flashing around and sent Longarm's nerves onto the razor's edge.

Another rag doll lay over there, a larger one. The thing that was there, scarlet with blood and torn or slashed into a nearly unrecognizable shapelessness, used to be a woman.

The thing, the woman, was still alive.

Longarm shoved the Colt back into his holster and hurried to kneel beside her.

He tried to freeze his face into an expressionless mask so that she would not see the revulsion that made him break into a cold sweat when he looked at her.

"I'm here, ma'am. I'll not hurt you." Gently, very gently, he reached out to smooth her hair, what was left of it, away from her ravaged face and to gentle her with a soft touch on the cheek.

The woman was depressing to look at. He simply refused to look at the dead, butchered children.

The woman's injuries were bad enough. She was mostly naked, although scraps of cloth on and around her showed that she must have been wearing a nightdress of some sort. Her torso was horribly gashed and mutilated. Her hands had been cut into shreds, and one leg was missing below the knee. She had been scalped, and both nostrils had been split. Random gashes dotted the rest of her pain-wracked body.

She was dying. She *had* to be dying. No one could possibly want to live after the abuses she had suffered, and Longarm hoped for her sake she would die quickly, before the shock of the attack wore off.

Incredible though it seemed to him, she was not only still alive at the moment, she was lucid and coherent in her thinking. She was able to listen to him and to ask, "Who are you?" in a burbling whisper that was distorted by a cut in her cheek.

"Deputy United States marshal, ma'am," Longarm said, still stroking and trying to soothe her.

"Thank God."

He had to bend closer to the gruesome sight in order to hear and understand her. He steeled himself and tried to show no reaction to the injuries. Surely she could not be aware of the extent of them or she could not—no one could—be so apparently calm, even taking into account the terrible shock that must be temporarily dulling the pain.

"Can you tell me who did this, ma'am?"

Her face twisted, and a single tear rolled out of the corner of one eye to mingle with the blood that was still fresh on her cheek. "Arlen," she whispered.

"Arlen, ma'am?"

"Arlen Cooper." Another tear fell. "My . . . my man. The children's daddy."

Longarm felt himself go cold inside. The name Arlen Cooper burned itself into his consciousness. If a man could do this to his own people . . .

"Came home drunk," the woman went on. "Been upset a long time. Dry-land farmin', you see. It's no good. Crops bad. No money." She snorted, and a pale pink bubble appeared at the place where her nose used to be. "Good crop three years in five, they said. We never seen a good crop. Been here six year come fall. Wore Cooper down, it did. Took the will right outa him. Drove him till he was purely crazy."

Longarm did not argue with her. The poor woman did not need that in her last moments. But any son of a bitch who could do something like this and be thinking clearly enough to try to cover it as an Indian attack was not all that crazy, in Longarm's opinion. A quitter, yes; an animal, certainly; but not crazy enough to disregard his own precious ass when he picked up the scythe or the butcher knife or whatever and set to chopping up his own kids.

"I'm glad you come, Marshal," Mrs. Cooper said.

"I'll do what I can, ma'am." This too, this ordinary if extraordinarily violent murder, was a matter for the local law's jurisdiction and not his. But he saw no reason to tell her about technicalities now. Besides, right now, viewing the devastation Arlen Cooper had left behind him early this morning, Deputy Marshal Custis Long did not feel any interest in observing those technicalities. If Long found

Cooper, the man would surely pay in the most basic of all possible ways.

There was a place in the Good Book where it said something about an eye for an eye and a tooth for a tooth. Longarm remembered that.

"Is there . . . anything I can do for you, ma'am?"

She tried to smile, although the pain was reaching her now. The shock was wearing off all too soon.

"You've come, Marshal. I . . . we . . . thank you."

Longarm hoped with everything that was in him that Mrs. Cooper had no knowledge of what had happened to her beloved children.

Her eyes had been bright, unnaturally bright. Now they began to dull and to film darkly. The life was slipping from her. The truly incredible thing was that she had managed to live long enough to tell him.

Longarm was fervently grateful that she had.

That need might well have been what kept her clinging to life as long as she had. Now the need was exhausted and so was she.

She gave him a thin effort at a smile and gestured feebly with her right wrist. Longarm suspected that she wanted to grasp his hand. She must not have known that she had no recognizable hand left there for him to hold.

The futility, the pain of not being able to give her the comfort she needed, brought a sharp sting to the back of Longarm's eyes, and he stroked her one undamaged cheek again, wishing that there was more he could do for her. There was not.

Mrs. Cooper sighed softly. The long, slow sigh turned into a lengthy exhalation that must have lasted all of thirty seconds.

She did not inhale again afterward.

It was ended.

Longarm stood, his legs weak and his stomach churning, and backed out of the soddy without allowing his eyes to focus on anything in it. As soon as he was outside he spun away from the broken door, bending and leaning forward.

There had been little left in his stomach from the previous night's meal at the Diamond F. By the time he was done retching there was nothing left at all, and he had a sour taste of bile in his mouth.

He leaned against the front wall of the still smouldering soddy and did not look up again until several minutes later, when he heard the sound of approaching hoofbeats.

There was a wagon pulling into the yard, a wagon filled with a man and a collection of young boys ranging in age from ten to somewhere in the upper teens. Behind the wagon were several other men and boys on saddle horses. Buckets and loose shovels rattled in the otherwise empty bed of the wagon. They were obviously neighbors drawn by the smoke, come to help if they could.

Longarm rushed into the yard to stop them there so the young ones would not be allowed close and so the men could prepare themselves for what they would now be expected to clean up.

The weather- and care-worn faces of the men turned hard when he told them, and the younger boys were quickly sent away.

"I'll need some help from you too," Longarm said.

"How's that, Marshal?" the oldest of the men, a farmer named Willis, asked.

"I need a description of Arlen Cooper and his horse, and what he would likely be wearing. Anything you can think to tell me."

One of the other men touched Willis at the elbow and cautioned him, "We don't know this man, Paul. An' Cooper's been a good neighbor all this time. There mought be things here we don't know of."

An icy calm steadied Longarm. He reached out with a slow, inexorable force and took the speaker by the throat. He turned the man and half carried him, gasping and choking and tottering on the tips of his toes, to the soddy door.

He shoved the man inside and took a fistful of hair on the top of his head, turning his face, his eyes, from one side of the cabin to the other. Longarm did not look. He had seen it already. He needed no reminders.

Then he snatched the man back from the doorway and threw him into the dirt.

The fellow offered no resistance. He rolled onto his stomach and came to his knees, gagging and spewing acid vomit onto the ground. The man's friends and neighbors turned their eyes away.

"Does anyone else want a look before we talk?" Longarm challenged in a cold, low voice.

No one else did.

Chapter 6

There was no way Longarm or anyone else could track Arlen Cooper across the hard, sun-baked expanse of the plains grassland. Marvelous feats of tracking were all very well and good for Natty Bumppo and the boys in another Cooper's *Leatherstocking Tales*. They might even have been possible in the moist and gentle forests of the East that that Cooper had written about. But here the soil, where it had not been broken by a damn-fool dry-farmer's plow, and all too often where it had been, was dry and hard and sere. A pawing buffalo had a hell of a time denting the surface, which was why the old wallows had been used year after year by countless generations of buffalo seeking relief from heat and sun and insects.

About all Longarm could do to try to catch up with Arlen Cooper was to guess where the man might have gone and haul ass in that direction after him.

Cooper's neighbors had had two guesses on that subject. Neither of them had to do with Denver.

"Old Arlen hated that city," one of them had said, unconsciously referring to his recent but now former neighbor in the past tense. "Said he couldn't abide the smell nor the city folks, neither one."

The two towns all the men agreed Cooper might have fled toward were Childs Ferry, a watering stop for the railroad on the banks of the South Platte, or Dry, which they said was little more than a watering spot of a different sort, with a saloon and a potbellied stove—"potbellied Injun hoor, too," one of the men had added with a laugh—northwest of the Cooper place.

Either could have been a possible hole-up place for Cooper, but Longarm was headed now toward Childs Ferry on the theory that he should check it first. If Cooper had gone to Dry it would still be possible to catch him later, while if he had headed for the river he would be able to jump a train and make the chase all that much more difficult.

As he rode Longarm breathed silent apologies to Carrie and Tom Smith. He had no time to be off chasing Arlen Cooper now.

Mrs. Cooper and the children were already dead. Nothing Longarm or any other peace officer could do now would ever bring them back to life.

But, damn it, Longarm had been the one to find those corpses. He had listened to Mrs. Cooper's last words. He had seen what was left of the children.

As a peace officer it was probably—hell, it *was*—his duty to report the murders to the local sheriff and let the matter be disposed of in the proper jurisdiction.

But as a man, by God, he could not ride on and give Arlen Cooper a chance to get away scot-free.

And he was very much afraid that if he did things by the book, that was exactly what could happen.

Regulation books be damned; the plain and simple truth of it was that every hour of freedom a felon had after the commission of his crime increased the fugitive's chances of making a clean getaway.

If a man was not caught in the act or damn close to it, he might never be caught at all.

In this wide, wide land where both time and news moved slowly, a man could be a complete stranger twenty miles from his doorstep. And here a man was known by whatever name he announced when he introduced himself.

Mrs. Cooper had said that her man went loco from the pressures of their hard life. Bullshit, Longarm thought. The son of a bitch had been sane enough to try to cover his crime with false Indian spoor. He hadn't done it worth a shit, but he had been sane and sensible enough to make the try.

So he was likely to be sane and sensible enough as well to go to ground under another name and in another place and think he could go right on with a better and less encumbered life than the wife and kids had permitted on that hardscrabble homestead.

The very idea of Arlen Cooper living to enjoy an unencumbered future made the bile rise in Longarm's throat again, and he bumped his rented horse from a lope into a canter to close the distance to Childs Ferry.

He reached the town by late morning, much sooner than he would have thought.

He knew, of course, that the South Platte and the railroad took a northward bend before lining out toward Julesburg and the Union Pacific main line, but he had not realized just how close to the Cooper place, and to the Smith homestead as well, the rails ran here. His mental map had been some miles off on that point, and he tucked the information away for future reference.

There was not much to Childs Ferry. Longarm had passed through it on the train many times without having cause to pay particular attention to it.

There was the inevitable railroad depot, little more than a shed with a roofed loading platform here, and the tall bulk of the water tank where the steam locomotives could draw their water. A single street with a handful of stores faced the tracks. There were a few houses and, at the near end of the town, a public livery barn with stockpens attached for those few farmers or local ranchers who might be wanting to load out stock here for the eastern markets.

It shouldn't take a hell of a long time to discover if Arlen Cooper was here.

Longarm went first to the railroad depot and checked with the agent/telegrapher.

Cooper could not be but a few hours ahead of Longarm, if that much. No one answering his description had taken the morning southbound to Denver. The northbound was not due through until mid-afternoon, and so far there were no passengers ticketed to depart from Childs Ferry.

A man did not necessarily need a ticket in order to ride the trains, though, and Longarm knew it. Cooper could still be in town, waiting for an opportunity to slip under a halted or slowing car for a free ride.

Longarm rode to the north end of the town and made a trip back down along the street, looking not for Arlen Cooper at the moment but for the bright sorrel cob the man would have been riding.

He did not see the horse tied along the street, so he went on down to the livery barn. The hostler, an unhurried man with the smell of cheap whiskey on his breath, was relaxing in a straight-backed chair tilted comfortably against the front wall of the place in the sunshine. He stood and nodded when Longarm reined to a halt in front of him.

"Howdy."

"Howdy yourself." Longarm dismounted and showed the man his badge. The hostler's eyebrows went up.

"Official business, Marshal?"

Longarm nodded. It was not exactly a lie. Until the local law took jurisdiction over the murders, it should be any peace officer's duty to apprehend the son of a bitch if possible.

The hostler grinned at him, and his rheumy eyes took on a faint sparkle. This was likely the most excitement he had had in ages. "Well, you ain't after me, 'cause I ain't done nothing that serious lately. So how c'n I help you?"

"Do you know a man named Arlen Cooper?"

The hostler shook his head. "Never heard of him."

Longarm described man and horse both. All he got for his efforts was a shake of the hostler's head. "I know for a fact he ain't brought the horse here. Haven't had a stranger for a customer for a week, I haven't. Haven't noticed anybody like that ride past neither, or I'd of remarked on it to myself."

"You notice things, do you?" Longarm asked.

The old fellow grinned, exposing tobacco-browned stubs where his teeth used to be. "I'm a nebby sort o' old shit. Admit it myself, I do. Might as well, 'cause if I don't there's plenty of others will tell it on me."

"Good," Longarm said with a smile. He turned away long enough to loosen the cinch of his McClellan and fetch out his bottle of Maryland rye. "Care for a friendly nip?" he offered.

The hostler's grin got bigger. "Since it's friendly offered, it wouldn't be friendly to refuse." He accepted the bottle and took a long pull on it, then carefully wiped the neck with his wrist before returning it to its owner.

Longarm took a pull too. The excellent rye spread heat through his gut, reminding him that he had not gotten around to breakfast yet and it was nearly time for lunch. Longarm corked the bottle and returned it to his saddlebag.

"I'd like to leave the horse here for an hour or so. Could be less. He hasn't been grained in a while, and he could use it. So could I, for that matter."

"I'll see to it," the hostler promised. "If it's all right with you I'll pull your gear an' give him a rubdown while I'm at it. Be restful for him, an' I take it you got to use him again today."

Longarm nodded.

"Only place in town you can find a nosebag for human persons is in that shanty over there," he said, pointing. "It's all right if you like fried grease."

Longarm thanked him and left. Before he went to the cafe for his overdue breakfast, he took a quick walk through town by way of the back alley behind the stores. There was no sign of Cooper, but he had wanted to make sure.

He stopped in at the town's one saloon as well, but the only customers in the place at this hour were a few old men who were drinking their lunch. Longarm wondered what the able-bodied local men did for a living. Of if there were any able-bodied local fellows, for that matter. The smell of sour beer and the fly-specked free lunch counter in the saloon were no temptation at all, so he backed out of the place and went on down to the cafe the hostler had pointed out to him.

"Hello." The serving girl in the little place was plain, but she was friendly enough.

There was life in Childs Ferry after all, Longarm decided. There were only four tables in the cafe, and two of them were already occupied by coffee drinkers when Longarm arrived. None of the men resembled the description he had been given of Arlen Cooper.

"What will you have?" the girl asked when Longarm was seated.

"Since I haven't eaten yet today, how about I get the two birds with one stone? A steak big enough to come over the edges of the plate, and cover the whole mess with fried eggs. Can you handle that?"

She smiled. She was much too drab for the change of

expression to make her pretty, but at least it made her seem a little less plain. "Does a dog have fleas?"

"Steak and eggs it'll be then, pretty lady."

The girl giggled and blushed and dashed off toward the back of the place. Longarm suspected he was about to get the very best they had to offer here.

In very little time, and feeling vastly better, he was back at the livery for his horse.

The hostler was still working on the animal. He had it inside the barn secured in cross-ties and was using a soft dandybrush to work on the animal's legs. Its back already gleamed from the grooming, and there was a heavy smell of liniment in the air.

"That didn't take you long," the hostler observed.

"Nope," Longarm agreed.

"Can you give me another couple minutes? I don't like to leave a job half done."

Longarm thought about the watch in his vest pocket, but left it alone. Another few minutes would not make that much difference, and he needed a moment or two to let the tensions unwind themselves. He propped an arm against the front wall of a box stall and pulled a cheroot from his pocket. "Mind if I smoke inside?"

The hostler squinted at him for a moment, then shrugged an assent. "You ain't drunk, and you don't look like an idjit. Just mind your match an' ashes, and it'll be all right."

Longarm thanked the man and lit up. The smoke tasted good after the meal.

While the hostler worked on his horse, moving quickly now, Longarm's glance drifted up and down the barn. Toward the front there were a few decrepit nags with harness marks on their front quarters. The box stalls were at the other end of the barn. There were six box stalls, only half of them occupied. Worn but well tended stock saddles hung on the walls of two of the stalls. The place was not much, but it was clean and tidy. The weed-straw bedding was fresh, and the odors of horseflesh and manure that filled the barn were unsoured. The livery almost certainly offered buggies and wagons to rent with the harness horses, but they were out of sight somewhere. Longarm felt himself relaxing for practically the first time since Carrie Smith had walked into Billy Vail's office.

The hostler finished brushing the horse's legs, cleaned the animal's feet, and insisted on resaddling for his customer.

"That'll be ten cents," he said when he was done.

Longarm paid the amount gladly. This break in Childs Ferry had not been productive, but it had sure as hell made him feel better.

"Could you direct me to Dry from here?" he asked when he was ready to go.

"Sure thing," the old hostler said. And he was, amazingly, able to give clear and concise instructions.

Longarm felt halfway human again when he rode away from the little town, even though he was achingly aware of the speed with which the hands of the Ingersoll were spinning inside his vest pocket.

Chapter 7

Childs Ferry had been small, but Dry was hardly recognizable as a settlement.

It had been built in the bottom of a hollow, where a pond of stagnant water collected during the spring melt and then quickly went away. Remaining traces of underground moisture had been enough to encourage the growth of a small stand of cottonwoods at some time in the past, but now only the gray skeletons of the trees were left. A few green sprigs showed lingering traces of life in the old trees and probably gave enough encouragement to save them so far from the woodbox.

Under a spread of bare branches there was a low, rock-walled building that was the saloon Longarm had been told about. A few yards away, on the edge of the grove, there were two cabins.

The three structures made up the entirety of Dry. Yet, oddly enough, there was more visible activity here than there had been back in Childs Ferry. A scantling pen held half a dozen saddle horses, and there were several wagons parked in the grove as well, their still hitched drafters dozing in the meager shade offered by the cottonwoods.

Longarm tied his horse to the outside of the pen rails and noticed that the saddle scabbards on the horses inside it were all empty. Apparently Dry was not the sort of place where a man could trust his things to stay there if he left them unattended. He took the hint and carried his Winchester with him when he went inside.

The saloon was busy, even though it was only the middle of a Saturday afternoon. Apparently a fair number of the men within riding distance gave themselves long weekends.

A group of men were standing at the bar with drinks before them. The drinks, Longarm noticed, were served in relatively unbreakable metal cups instead of fragile glass.

A card game of some sort was going on in a back corner of the place, and there was a dark-haired, very dark-skinned woman with sagging breasts and a rounded paunch trying to arouse the passions of a solitary drinker who sat morose and silent at another of the tables.

Longarm paused inside the doorway to let his eyes adjust to the dim shade inside the almost windowless saloon after the bright sunshine outdoors. The Winchester hung inoffensively in his left hand. Other rifles and saddle carbines were propped here and there along the walls or against the front of the bar.

It took only moments for his vision to become clear. No one inside the place matched the description he had been given of Arlen Cooper.

He mouthed a cussword to himself and took a step forward, intending to have a quiet word with the proprietor of the place. In a hog ranch like this one it was seldom wise to make loud announcements about one's affiliation with the law.

"Longarm! M' ol' pal." The glad cry came loud and clear from the far corner where the card game was in progress.

Longarm looked that way. It was the cowboy from down at the Diamond F. Although what the kid would be doing all the way up here, Longarm did not know.

The Diamond F hand was about three sheets before the wind and into the giggling stage. When he saw Longarm he tried to get out of his chair and turn to face Longarm at the same time. The maneuver was too much for him and he stumbled, banging into the edge of the table where he had been sitting with his back to the door when Longarm entered, and splashing part of a drink into another player's lap.

The offended card player tried to push back from the table in too much of a hurry. He too had had more than enough whiskey. He lost his balance and went over backward into the filth that littered the floor.

The rest of the players found the whole thing to be a source of hilarity, and they began to hoot and holler.

Longarm shook his head, half amused and half disgusted. He started toward the table, intending to speak to the cowboy, but he was stopped in mid-stride by the cold, rolling clack of a hammer being cocked.

He felt a chill in his gut.

While his attention had been on the card table and the Diamond F cowboy, the lone drinker at the table had come to his feet.

The man looked frightened. His face had gone suddenly pale, and he was holding the Indian whore in front of him like a shield.

He had a revolver cocked in his right hand while he held the woman by the throat with his left. The cold steel muzzle of the gun was shoved into the whore's ear.

"Don't you move another step, you son of a bitch," the man said. His voice was quavering and he had begun to sweat. He looked like he was on the thin edge of control and was quickly slipping over to the ugly side of that edge.

"Something wrong?" Longarm asked mildly.

"Don't you move," the man warned again.

The interior of the saloon had gone suddenly and completely silent. The men at the bar were swallowing with nervous difficulty, and one man was trying to slip out of sight behind the protective barrier of the bar. The card players were frozen in place, even the man who had been rolling on the floor beside his tipped-over chair.

The barman held a double-barreled shotgun in his fists. The gun had wickedly short barrels. If the saloon keeper was fool enough to touch off even one of the triggers, the spread of shot from that handspan barrel would be wide enough to bloody half of his patrons of the moment.

Longarm froze into position. He had no idea what in hell was going on here, but he had no desire to trigger a blood-bath that could likely eliminate the population of Dry completely by the time the smoke cleared.

He smiled, seemingly calm and unruffled. "Is there something I can do for you, neighbor?"

The man with the gun licked dry lips. He was trembling visibly, the barrel of the revolver stabbing roughly against the side of the Indian woman's head. Her eyes were wide with terror, but she had enough presence of mind to hold herself rigid in her captivity.

"I know you, you son of a bitch," the man said. "You're the one they call the Long Arm of the Law, ain't you? Course you are." He squeezed his eyes shut for a moment, then opened them wide. "Oh, Jesus. But you ain't gonna take me, Longarm. One move an' I'll blow this woman's head off. I swear I will."

"I'm not moving," Longarm said softly.

He looked at the man more closely, trying to match the face to the Wanted posters that had accumulated for years in the Justice Department offices.

He was certain he had never seen a picture or a drawing of this man's face. It was always possible, of course, that a written description had been circulated, but those were always uncertain at best and usually were only the vaguest of word sketches.

A man of middling height, dark-haired, thirty to thirty-

78

five years, no visible marks or scars. That description would tally with half of the Wanted flyers that came in. The man could be anyone, fleeing from any damned thing.

"I have no quarrel with you, friend," Longarm said in a soft, soothing tone. "I don't know who you are, and I didn't come here for you."

"Oh, Jesus," the man repeated. His voice was as shaky as his gun hand.

The whore was trembling now too. The man's grip on her throat was pulling her up on her tiptoes, and her legs were getting weak. Her quivering made her floppy tits wobble under the thin shift that covered her flaccid body.

"Oh, Jesus," the gunman said.

"Why don't you release the lady," Longarm suggested. "I didn't come here for you," he repeated.

It was the truth.

It was also true, of course, that now that the man had shown himself, Longarm's duty was clear. He would have to apprehend the poor bastard now, whether he wanted to or not. He was careful to make no promises about that that he would not be able to keep.

"You're lyin'," the gunman said.

Longarm smiled and shook his head. "If you know enough about me to know who I am, then you've likely heard enough about me to know that I don't lie. I'll play you straight, friend—whoever you are."

The man looked like he wanted to cry. "You really didn't..."

Longarm shook his head again.

"What the fuck is goin' on here," the barman demanded loudly. He was still holding the shotgun, but he looked unsure of who he intended to turn it on.

"Deputy United States marshal," Longarm said.

The Diamond F cowboy dropped into a cross-legged

sitting position on the dirty floor, his liquor-weakened legs unable to hold him any longer. "Tha's right," he asserted for them all to hear. "M' ol' pal Longarm. Bes' damn Yew Ess deppity in the hull damn country." He hiccupped and grinned, a bit of drool running down onto his chin. He did not seem to notice. At least, he made no attempt to wipe the spittle away.

Longarm was pleased to see the twin muzzles of the barman's scattergun swing a fraction of an inch toward the gunman. In an out-of-the-way hog ranch there was always some doubt about where the sympathies of the management might lie. A place like this was not likely to have a clientele that found the law high on their praise list.

"You got to give me a chance," the gunman said.

"All right," Longarm agreed. He did not allow any uncertainty to show in his voice.

"You got to let me get away," the gunman amended.

Longarm sighed. "You know I can't promise you that," he said. "But you let the woman go, and you'll get your fair chance. I can give you that much."

The gunman's eyes squeezed closed again in despair, and for a moment Longarm thought he was going to make good on his threat. The man's knuckles were white on the butt of his revolver, and Longarm thought surely he was going to send a bullet into the whore's brain.

"Maybe it isn't as bad as you think," Longarm said softly. "I still don't know who you are. I have no idea what you've done. It could be you're looking at a little time away from folks and then you can go back to being loose." He smiled. "Think about that."

"I can't do it, Longarm," the man said. His voice was a little firmer now. Some of the trembling seemed to have subsided.

"You don't know that, friend. Let the woman go, and we'll see what we can work out. If nothing else, I can testify in court then that you cooperated with me at the time of arrest. That could be enough to make things easier on you."

"You don't know," the man wailed.

"Exactly," Longarm said with a smile. "That's what I've been trying to tell you. So let the woman go, and we'll see what we can work out."

"No!" the gunman snapped. His grip closed tighter on the Indian woman's throat, and she rolled her eyes as she was pulled almost off her feet by the desperate man's hold.

"What is it you've done?" Longarm asked.

"Kilt a man," the gunman said. "Son of a bitch deserved it, even if I was drunk at the time."

"You won't get any six-month sentence, then," Longarm argued, "but you might not have to swing for it. You'd still be alive, man. You could try for a pardon. I can't make you any promises, but such things happen. You could still live to walk the streets a free man."

The gunman shook his head violently from side to side, unconsciously shaking the woman as he did so. She looked ready to faint. He looked ready to cry.

"You don't understand," the gunman said. "He was a rich son of a bitch. They'd hang me for it back in Kaintuck."

"Who are you?" Longarm asked. It was better to keep the man talking than to let him start shooting, he figured.

"Wallace," he said. "Jace Wallace."

Longarm tried to recall the name from among the hundreds in the Wanted file, but he could not. "That name doesn't mean anything to me, Jace. It must have been a long time ago."

"It was."

"There are no flyers out on you now, Jace. There's been

time for the blood to cool. It might not go as bad on you as you think. Let the woman go, and we'll see if we can't work something out."

"I—"

The Indian woman's legs gave out. Her eyes rolled upward until the dark pupils disappeared, and she fell into a dead faint. Jace Wallace still had a firm grip on her throat. His arm was locked. When she fell she dragged him down after her, the muzzle of the revolver still pressed firmly into her ear.

Longarm felt his stomach flipflop as his hand sped toward the big Colt that rode on his belt.

Jace Wallace's revolver spat flame and thunder. Longarm was sure the man had not meant to fire, that his trigger finger was jostled when the whore pulled him down to the floor with her, but there was no help for it now.

Blood blossomed bright and fresh on the side of her head, and she sprawled flat on the floor, giving Longarm a clear shot at the terrified gunman who had admitted to one killed and now looked to have a second one on his conscience.

Longarm's Colt roared and rocked back in his hand, and a spot of red little larger than a dime appeared in the center of Jace Wallace's forehead. Wallace's lifeless body fell face down on top of the Indian woman's body.

The stink of burnt gunpowder in close confinement was strong inside the saloon, overpowering the other smells of the place.

Longarm spun to face the rest of the men in the place, taking no chances. Jace Wallace might have had friends here, or some of these jaspers might just want an opportunity to backshoot a lawman on general principles.

No one else had moved, including the barman.

A stony silence held for several long moments as the sounds of the gunshots hung in the air. The barkeep broke the mood by letting the hammers of his scattergun down to safe-cock and slowly replacing the vicious little weapon out of sight beneath the bar.

Someone else coughed nervously, and the Diamond F cowboy who had unwittingly started the whole thing chortled with pleasure at having seen his good and true pal at work. Longarm shuddered. He had not wanted this, still did not, but he had been given no choice.

He holstered the Colt and went over to the two bodies on the floor.

Jace Wallace would never have to fear pursuit from the law again. Whatever the extent of his crime, whoever it had been who died at his hand, the debt was cancelled now. Tha back of his head was an unrecognizable pulp.

Longarm lifted him off the whore and pushed his body aside. He expected to see a very similar sight when he looked at the paunchy, unwholesome whore, but he did not.

Somehow during the fall Wallace's gun had been twisted out of its nest inside the woman's ear.

The gun had gone off. There was bleeding. A rather great deal of bleeding.

But now Longarm could see that very little damage had actually been done to her.

Likely she would lose the hearing in that ear for a time and quite possibly for the rest of her life. But at least she did have a rest-of-her-life to look forward to. The copious flow of bright blood was coming from a tear Wallace's bullet had gouged out of the lobe of her ear. The damage was no worse than that.

"B'Gawd," the Diamond F cowboy's drunken buddy yelped. "Ol' Wallace give her an underbite." He and the others around the card table began to chuckle and then to roar.

One of the men who had been at the bar began to sidle

toward the front door, his ears, unmarked, a glowing red from blood that was not spilling. As he turned his back toward the other men in the room and headed in a crabbing scuttle toward the front door, Longarm saw the reason for his retreat. It had nothing to do with a fear of the law like Jace Wallace's had been. The man had pissed his pants. Longarm pretended he did not see.

The barman settled things down some by placing a jug of cheap whiskey on top of the bar and calling loudly, "On the house, boys."

The men in the place crowded around the jug of free whiskey, and the barman left his post and came out from behind the bar to help Longarm.

He brought a damp rag with him and used it to wipe the whore's forehead and clean up some of the blood on her shoulder, ignoring the dead patron on the floor.

"You tried," the man said. "Reckon I got to thank you for that. An' you did save ol' Weechi here."

Longarm could not see that he had accomplished all that much by his own efforts, if he intended to be truthful about the matter. The woman had simply gone and fainted. From there on out it had just been the roll of the dice. Still, the woman—Weechi? He wondered what kind of name or nickname that was supposed to be—was alive. There was that to be thankful for.

"I'm just sorry it happened," he said honestly.

"You could've taken him. Could've said you'd let him go and then gunned him as he went for the door. I could see it in his eyes that he just wanted to get clear somehow."

"I could have taken him that way," Longarm admitted, "and lost a dozen others like him by having to shoot men I'd otherwise be able to talk into cuffs when the word got around that I'd broke a promise."

The barkeep mulled that for a moment, then grunted.

Longarm had no idea if the sound was intended to convey agreement or disgust.

"Something official bring you here, Deputy?" the man asked.

"Yes. I'm looking for a man. Not Jace Wallace. A fellow who might have been in here this morning."

The barman looked over his shoulder toward where the patrons were still crowding happily around the free whiskey. He jerked his head toward a side room and said, "He'p me get Weechi in there, and I'll tell you if I can. No point in advertisin' it, though."

"All right."

The woman was regaining consciousness, but she was in no condition to walk. The two men raised her to her feet and, one on either side of her, half carried and half dragged her into the room the barman indicated.

Longarm helped the man put her down on top of the blankets of a cot that had all the appeal and the smell of a coyote den. Longarm guessed that this was her place of business and residence combined, although he would have thought it inhumane to make a hound stay in such quarters. He tried to close his senses to the odors.

"What is it now, Deputy?" the barman asked.

"The man's name is Arlen Cooper," Longarm said.

The barman shook his head. The name meant nothing to him. "How's he look?"

Longarm told him.

The man snapped his fingers and said, "Sure, he was here. Late mornin' it was. Stayed to have himself some drinks and a bite to eat. You only missed him by three, four hours or so."

"Damn," Longarm mumbled. "Did he say much while he was here?"

"Funny you should ask that, but he sure was wound up,

tight as a two-bit watch. Seemed kinda jumpy and real talkative, like he couldn't keep his mouth shut if he wanted. Which he sure didn't."

Longarm reached for a cheroot and offered one to the barman, who accepted with pleasure. When the cigars were lighted, Longarm asked, "Could you try to remember anything the man said, please? Anything at all could be a help."

"Hell, that's easy. I had to listen to it enough. Gets to be a trial listenin' to a bunch of drunk assholes spout off about their problems, let me tell you. But don't mention I said that, if you please."

"I won't," Longarm promised.

"Anyhow, this fella . . . he never gave a name, but it sure sounds like the one you want . . . he was in here, just like I said. Had him a pocketful of hard money that he was braggin' he'd won someplace or other."

That was interesting, Longarm thought. It wasn't the grind of poverty that had gotten to the son of a bitch, then. It was a sudden affluence instead. He felt a quick resurgence of grief for poor Mrs. Cooper. She had died never knowing.

"He was stuffing his face like he hadn't eat in days," the barman was going on, "and knocking back the drinks pretty regular too. Couldn't seem to hold still in no fashion. He was bragging it up about this money he'd won an' sayin' something about a lady friend that he'd be damn sure getting close to now."

"Did he give any idea where this lady friend might be?"

The barkeep got a sly expression on his puffy face and chortled, "The guy never named no names, you understand, but I hear more'n folks might think when I'm behind that bar. Yeah, I know where he's going. From what he said, the woman pretty much's got to be Harriet Swann. Widder Swann, she calls herself, but nobody I know of knows anything about there ever bein' a mister."

"You're sure of that?" Longarm asked. "It could be important."

The barman shrugged. "'Bout as sure as I could be without him sayin' her name."

"Do you know where this Widow Swann lives?"

"I do. Reckon I could tell you. Just don't tell nobody how you came to hear."

"You can count on it," Longarm said.

"All right, then." The barman gave Longarm directions to the Widow Swann's place, which was north and east from Dry and convenient to a railroad whistlestop called Dukes Crossing.

Too damned convenient to the rails, Longarm thought. If Cooper had gotten enough found money for the two of them to take off with, they could all too easily take a train for fresh country. That certainly seemed probable, instead of him settling in again so close to where his family was murdered and he mysteriously disappeared.

Longarm pulled the Ingersoll from his vest and checked the time. He thought back to when the agent in Childs Ferry had said the northbound would be through, then added time for it to travel from there on to Dukes Crossing.

He felt a measure of relief. There would not be time for Cooper to go from here to the Swann place and then on to Dukes Crossing in time for them to get the afternoon connection. They probably would not be there until some time tomorrow at the earliest.

And if they took more time to get involved in some serious belly bumping, they might choose to lay up there for a while before they ventured out again.

There was a good possibility of that too, Longarm thought. Arlen Cooper would have no idea that anyone was onto him yet. He had left the false Indian spoor behind. He would likely think himself free and clear and able to have his fun with the Widow Swann all he wanted.

Bastard, Longarm thought.

The killing of Mrs. Cooper and her children, *his* children too, was as cold a thing as Longarm had ever come on when it was seen in this light.

The son of a sorry bitch had been *excited,* for Christ's sake. Eager. Actually *pleased* with himself.

Longarm thanked the barkeep and turned to leave, but the man stopped him with a touch on the elbow.

"Ol' Weechi's coming around now," he said.

"Yes?"

"I was thinkin' you might want to hump her. I mean, you saved her for me an' all that." He grinned. "Free, too. I wouldn't charge you for her. A quickie, that is." He chuckled. "Aw, hell, since it's you, why, I wouldn't charge you nothing even if you want somethin' fancy like."

Longarm looked down at the filthy, stinking bed and the whore who lay on it. His stomach rolled over at the thought of putting it anywhere *near* her. It was clear from smell alone that she hadn't bathed since the last time she forded a deep creek.

"Uh, it's nice of you to make the offer, but I'd better get after Cooper now."

"Yeah, well, if you change your mind, Longarm, you jus' stop back by here. Any time. I figure I owe you one, and I pay my debts."

"Thanks," Longarm said.

He hurried out of there fast, not even taking time to speak to the Diamond F cowhand who was his great and good buddy.

Chapter 8

Longarm was cursing and fit to kick a dog, if he saw one. That was damned well unlikely because, following the directions the barman back in Dry had given him, he couldn't find *anything*. Not the Widow Swann's house. Not a dog to kick. Nothing.

The man had been genuinely trying to be helpful. Longarm was convinced of that. If he were not, Longarm would be heading back there to kick *him*. But, damnation, he gave terrible directions. Longarm wished it had been the old hostler back in Childs Ferry he'd been asking. At least that fellow had known what he was doing when he said or did something.

Longarm looked toward the setting sun, off toward the distant mountain peaks that angled westward above Denver and here were barely visible, and felt urgency pull at his empty gut. That fine combined breakfast and lunch back in Childs Ferry was a long way behind.

It was not the hunger that was bothering him, though. He could put up with that for as long as it took. It was this miserable delay he was having in finding the Widow Swann's house.

He did not have time to mess around like this.

Arlen Cooper was out there somewhere in the dusk, happily congratulating himself on having gotten away with a savage form of butchery that would have gagged a self-respecting maggot.

And Tom Smith, Jr. was still scheduled to die the first thing Monday morning.

Longarm rode on, absolutely refusing to consult the Ingersoll in his vest, but practically able to feel every single tick the watch made.

He topped one low rise after another, each time hoping against hope that the Widow Swann's place would somehow magically sail into view in front of him. But, rise after rise, it did not.

He wanted to boot the horse into a lathering run, but did not. Cruelty was not only abhorrent, it would be stupid. He had to save the horse's strength. Whatever else might or might not happen, this night was going to be a long one. He would need the animal's strength for long-term use and could not spend it all in some futile burst of frustrated speed.

So he held a tight rein on himself, kept the animal moving at a saving gait, and felt the acids boil in his stomach.

A hint of movement caught his eye in the late dusk off to his right, and he turned his mount toward it. He stood in his stirrups. He was not sure, but . . .

A windmill. The movement he had seen was the slowly spinning vanes of someone's windmill. From where he had been he had been able to catch only a faint glimpse of the top of the mill.

Now, as he came nearer, he could see the full flower of the turning mill, then the tower, finally the small ranch house and yard where the well had been put down.

The Widow Swann's, Longarm thought. *At last.*

He rode a little closer, moving in a broad sweep to come up behind the house, and dismounted while he was still several hundred yards out.

It was nearly full dark now, and there were lights glowing inside the house. There were windows at the back of the place, but anyone inside would be in the lamplight. It was unlikely that those inside could see him unless they were alert enough to be keeping a serious watch for company.

He hobbled the horse and pulled its bridle so it could crop at the short grass while he was away, then took the Winchester from his scabbard and began a slow stalk toward the back of the house.

He soft-footed his way through the prairie grasses to the back of the house, grateful that the Widow Swann was not a dog fancier. Aside from the fact that he did not really want to find a dog to kick now, he damn sure did not want his presence announced.

It was too dark to get much of a look at the horses in the nearby corral, so he took it on faith that Cooper's mount would be there. It had to be there. He made his way quietly to the back of the house.

This one was no haphazard soddy. The house was not large, but it had been built with care and skill by someone who went to the expense and trouble of hauling milled lumber in from some distant source. There certainly was no usable timber anywhere near. Even the cottonwoods that grew along the course of the South Platte were useless for lumber.

The place was painted too, which was almost startling out here on the Empty. Most who came here to live were looking to make their fortunes from a start at rock bottom. Few who came here genuinely believed that they were fated for the fortunes they sought. Most came in desperation of one kind or another and went to little trouble about dwelling places they might have to abandon at the next drought or locust swarm or winter die-up.

The Widow Swann, Longarm thought, was a rare bird.

He reached the back wall of the house without alarming anyone inside and crouched there to listen, leaning the Winchester against the wall under a window.

He took a long look around at the little he could see in the poor light of the early evening, then closed his eyes and concentrated on his sense of hearing.

No one was talking inside. No one was moving about. Yet there was a faint undertone of some kind that he could detect only enough to become aware of. He could not make out what it was.

Not at first.

He listened intently, letting his breathing slow and deepen.

Breathing. He smiled. That was it. Someone was breathing in there. And, judging from the faint sound of it, they were breathing slowly and regularly in the pattern of a light sleep.

The sound seemed to be coming from only a few feet away from Longarm's head. At any other window he would have been able to hear nothing.

He paused to consider for a moment. The Widow Swann, and presumably Arlen Cooper as well, seemed to be taking an early evening nap.

Longarm listened more closely, but he could not hear the man's snoring.

It could be, then, that Cooper was not sleeping in the bedroom next to the widow lady. That meant that he might instead be in one of the front rooms, perhaps reading a magazine, or a railroad timetable. Or simply sitting there and contemplating with pleasure his own high intelligence in being able to rid himself of an unwanted family.

Longarm felt his blood heat as visions of Arlen Cooper rolled through his imagination.

Whatever the son of a bitch was doing, Longarm needed to find him before he chose a point to go busting inside. He dropped to his hands and knees and crawled silently to the next window, then on to the next.

He could hear nothing at any of them.

At the front window he stopped and raised himself slowly upright until his cheek was pressed against the freshly painted wood trim around the sash. The window was open, but he could hear nothing from it. Nothing at all. Surely if the man was in there he should be able to hear *something*.

Longarm took the Colt from his holster and held it ready while he leaned to the side, ever so slowly, and took a look inside the house.

He was at the parlor. An oil lamp burned on a table at the side of a plump upholstered sofa. A matching chair stood empty on the other side of the table. Lace doilies covered the arms and the backs of the furnishings. The place was tidy and decidedly feminine.

Nowhere, though, could Longarm see anything of Arlen Cooper.

He made a complete circuit of the house, repeating his Peeping Custis performance at each window now, except the bedroom opening where he knew there was someone inside.

He came up empty at each and every place.

So the only room where Cooper could be was in that bedroom. The son of a bitch *had* to be there.

He was not in a deep sleep either, or the sound of his breathing would have given him away.

As soon as Longarm made his entrance, then, the sleepers would be disturbed.

Longarm stood beside the open window for several moments, going through every action and activity in his mind, planning out every move he would have to make, visualizing the responses Arlen Cooper was apt to make, preparing himself as best he could for each possibility.

He would have liked to have had someone with him to cover the front door while Longarm made his unannounced entry at the back. But he was alone, and he would have to take the man alone. He damn sure was not going to back off now and give Cooper any opportunities to slip away again.

Longarm made sure of his grip on the Colt and steeled himself, ready to spring.

There was no screen mesh covering the window. The sash had been pushed high to catch the afternoon breeze, but soon the night chill would wake the sleepers and make them lower the window. At the moment, though, lacy wisps of curtain swayed to what was left of the late-day currents.

Longarm took a deep breath, poised himself, and jumped.

He leaped through the window with an ear-splitting shriek that was calculated to confuse and demoralize whoever was inside. He hit the floor on his shoulder, tucking his head low and to one side, and rolled ass over toenails and back to his feet.

The Colt came up aimed square at the pillows at the head of the bed.

A green-eyed girl with red hair flowing down over milky and quite naked breasts sat bolt upright in her bed with a scream of terror at the sounds and the sight that had yanked her from her sleep.

Her eyes went wide as she took one look at the intruder in her bedchamber, and she fainted dead away.

Longarm looked frantically on the floor at the far side of the bed. He looked under the bed. He raced from one room of the house to another.

But there was no sign of Arlen Cooper.

Rarely had Deputy U. S. Marshal Custis Long felt so damnably, miserably, utterly embarrassed.

He had made a fine sneak and a swift, sure attack on the wrong house.

The place he had so carefully assaulted in the early night

was the home of Howard and Wilda Emry. The Emrys were not at home this weekend. They seemed to have gone to southern Wyoming for the funeral of an old friend. The house was, however, occupied by their visiting niece.

Longarm stammered out his apologies for probably the twentieth time as the girl, whose name was a most unappealing Emma Emry, came into the parlor, wrapping her uncle's outsized bathrobe around her.

Her visitor might be, and was, made uncomfortable by the circumstances of his entrance, but she seemed calm and even serene now that the initial shock was past. She finished tying the belt to the robe and began to brush her hair.

Longarm's embarrassment was fading too now. The damned filly *had* to know the effect she was creating. That floppy bathrobe gaped open at the throat and the lamplight caught the long, loose flow of her dark red hair as she brushed it. Her breasts rose to press high and perky against the covering cloth with every lift of her arms.

Longarm gave her a searching look—a rather pleasant endeavor, actually—and guessed that Miss Emma Emry was a spoiled girl, and quite probably a rich one as well.

Toothsome, though, he thought with a grin, remembering the pale, pear-shaped thrust of those breasts. He had gotten an unavoidable good look at them when he went back to the bedroom to rouse her from her faint, and the memory of them was enough to cause excess salivation.

Nor was that the extent of the girl's appeal. He guessed her age to be in the neighborhood of twenty, give or take a bit.

He had no idea how she normally wore all that red hair, but he damn sure liked it long and flowing the way it was now. It cascaded down on either side of a small face with clearly defined nose and chin and cheekbones, very full lips, heavy eyebrows a shade or two darker than her hair, and eyes as green as gemstones. Her eyelashes were very long and very dark, so much so that he suspected she did something artificial to make them that way.

Not that he was holding the artifice against her. On the whole, he had to admit that she was something better than merely presentable.

"Why are you smiling, Marshal? And looking at me like that? I insist that you stop, do you hear?" The words were those of a rebuke, but he noticed that there was more than a hint of coyness in the tone of voice. And she did not stop brushing her hair while she spoke. The sharp points of her nipples continued to slide up and down beneath the cloth of her uncle's bathrobe.

There would have been other, more appropriate attire available to her, he reflected. Not only did she have to know that he could see what her figure was doing to that cloth, she had to be able to feel the teasing scrape of it herself. The damned girl was deliberately playing with him.

Longarm grinned, his teeth white against the brown of his tanned face and full moustache.

"You didn't answer me," she snapped. This time she stopped brushing her hair. The result of that was not so bad either. The front of the robe had been pulled high and now was hung on the belt tie, making the front of it gap open even more than it had, and perhaps more than she realized. She was about to fall out of the thing, or at least selected portions of her were.

Longarm chuckled quietly to himself. Wherever she came from—and he was betting on someplace fancy way the hell back East—she was used to having the young men roll over and beg whenever she batted her eyes. Time she learned that it didn't always work that way out here in the real world.

He helped himself to a seat in one of the overstuffed

chairs, which was less comfortable than it looked, and pulled out a cheroot without asking her permission. He lighted the cigar and drew deep on the smooth flavor of the smoke.

"You didn't answer me," she repeated.

"Didn't need to," he said gently, but with a devilish grin. "You know mighty well why men look at you." He tilted his head to the side and stared at her, deliberately avoiding her face and openly assessing what he could see of her fine body. Which was enough, if considerably less than he had been able to see just a short while earlier.

"Not bad," he mused aloud. "A little on the light side for my taste, but not bad."

"Oh!" She looked shocked, as if she had never been spoken to like that before, and probably she had not. "You!" She stamped her foot once in exasperation. The foot was bare, though, and unprotected, the floor of the house bare and quite hard. It must have hurt. She managed to contain the yelp that threatened to leap out of her throat, but the pain showed on her face, which only made her all the angrier. "You!" she sputtered again.

Longarm laughed. "Where are you from, Emma?"

She flounced onto the thick cushions of the sofa in a pout. Longarm waited patiently, as if all of this was quite normal, and after a moment she answered, "Annapolis." She raised her chin archly and added, "That, sir, for your information, is in Maryland."

"Thank you," he said politely and took another pull on the cheroot.

Annapolis. That would explain some of it, then. All of those not-quite-eligible young men at the Naval Academy, all of them circumspect and proper and formal as hell. They had to be, at least when anybody was looking, or they'd get the boot.

On the other hand, if they were anything like the young

fellows with the ramrods up their butts at the other academy up in New York State, those boys could likely be wild and wooly when the chances came.

Longarm grinned at her again.

"And what, sir, is that supposed to mean?" she demanded.

"Nothing." He felt at ease now, but he had played long enough here. He stood and reached for the hat he had laid aside.

The girl quickly stood too. "You aren't going, are you?"

He nodded. "Got to get down the road."

In spite of her show of anger a moment or two before, she looked genuinely disappointed. She had been enjoying the game.

"I have supper in the oven," she said. "I was just waiting for it to cook when I drifted off. And then you came bursting in and frightened me half to death. There's enough for two." She sounded like she genuinely wanted him to stay.

Longarm's stomach responded to the invitation before he could refuse it. His stomach gurgled and rolled at the thought of a hot meal before he went on and once again tried to find the elusive Widow Swann's place.

"Please?" she asked. All of her pretense and haughtiness had been set aside now. She was young and frightened and lonely, and she truly wanted him to stay and eat with her.

"All right," he said. He really had intended to refuse the offer, but the acceptance was out of his mouth before he realized he was going to give it.

"Wonderful." She meant it. A smile of honest pleasure transformed her from a pretty girl into a truly lovely one, and she ran quickly into the kitchen to begin preparing the table with a second place setting.

Longarm put his hat down again and wandered into the

kitchen behind her. Watching her there would not be hard to take.

The meal was some sort of casserole thing, popular in the East perhaps but uncommon here, with the meat and vegetables and other truck all cooked together. He had to admit that it tasted considerably better than it looked.

While they ate, Emma went on a talking binge. She chattered at him about her home, her family, her suitors, talking non-stop while Longarm ate. The girl barely picked at her food. She seemed much more interested in the opportunity to talk with this tall and exceptionally handsome man who had so violently invaded her boudoir. From the things she said it was clear that he was totally different from anyone she had ever encountered before.

When he was done with the meal, Longarm pushed his plate away and shoved his chair back from the table.

Emma was on her feet and around to his side of the table before he could rise. She laid a hand on his arm to stop him from leaving.

"Yes?" he asked.

She dropped her eyes away from his and licked her lips nervously. Then she looked up at him. She was shorter than he had realized. The top of her auburn head barely came to his chin.

"What is it, Emma?"

She took a half step backward away from him, paused for a moment to get control of herself, then boldly lifted her chin and looked him in the eyes.

"This," she whispered.

She tugged once at the knot she had made in the belt at her waist and shrugged her shoulders. The bathrobe slipped off her and fell to the floor with a soft whisper of sound.

She stood before him, naked and beautiful, yet there was

a measure of uncertainty in her eyes.

Her figure was fine, the waist small, hips lightly swelling. Her legs were slim and shapely. The curly patch of hair at her vee, dark against the exceptional paleness of her lightly blue-veined skin, proved the authenticity of her hair color.

"Are you . . ." she licked her lips again and ducked her head so that soft wings of glossy hair hung down over her breasts ". . . offended?" She looked up at him, obviously quite worried about his response to this extraordinary offer.

Longarm's answer was a gentle smile, and she rushed forward into his arms.

Chapter 9

"I . . . I have a confession." She turned her head away from him. They were in the bedroom, both naked now, side by side on the narrow bed. She still seemed nervous, and Longarm was being patient with her, stroking and petting and kissing her slowly.

"Yes?"

"It might . . . disgust you. You might not . . . want me after I tell you."

"I doubt that, but go ahead."

"Before . . . before I fell asleep. You know, before you came flying through the window screaming at me like that." She smiled a little now at the thought of it, although she certainly had not been smiling at the time. "Well, what I'd come in here for after I put my dinner in the oven . . . the reason I wasn't wearing anything, you see . . ."

"It's all right," Longarm assured her, kissing her shoulder and leaning forward to roll her pink nipple over his tongue.

Emma blushed. "I know that is a terrible thing to do," she confessed. "I know that. But sometimes I can't stop myself. I know I shouldn't do it, but . . . it feels so *good*."

Longarm chuckled and drew her to him. He kissed her deeply, muttering low reassurances, and let his tongue drift slowly south, ringing first one breast and then the other, laving one nipple and then the next.

Down over the pale softness of her belly, into the dense

patch of auburn hair. Emma moaned and opened herself to him.

"Let's see if this is as good," he suggested.

"Cus . . . Custis. Oh, my. Oh, *my!*"

Her hips began to move of their own volition, pulsing softly to the flickering touch of him. She put a hand on the back of his head and kneaded her fingers into his dark brown hair, pressing him harder and harder against herself.

Longarm responded, driving her into mad spasms of raw need, making her body buck and leap under his touch. Emma stiffened and shuddered, arching her back and raising her pelvis to him. She cried out from the intensity of her feelings and became as rigid as a beautifully curved statue.

When the ecstasy was past she went completely limp, collapsing onto the sheets with a low, glad sigh.

"Well?" he asked, turning so that he lay beside her with her head nestled in the hollow of his shoulder.

"What, dear?"

"Was that as good?" he asked with a grin.

Emma sighed. "It was the most *wonderful* thing I've ever experienced. Truly it was, dear. But of course you already know that. You just want to hear me say it. Well, all right. I'm saying it, Mr. Deputy Marshal Custis Long. You are *wonderful*. I loved it. Every delicious second of it." She sighed again. "I never knew it could be so nice. I really didn't."

"Oh, but the nicest part is still to come," he assured her.

"Truly?"

"Uh-huh."

She smiled. "I can't wait for you to show me."

He stroked her gently, running his fingertips lightly over the sensitive flesh, rolling hard nipples between thumb and forefinger, enjoying the velvet texture of her skin.

Emma moaned again and opened herself to his touch.

She spread her milky-white thighs apart for him, and he raised himself over her, kneeling between her knees but still taking his time with her. It was obvious that she was inexperienced, and he did not want to rush or to hurt her.

Emma raised her hips to him eagerly, pushing herself up onto him until he was deep within her.

Her eyes drooped and then closed, and she bit at her underlip as waves of pleasure washed through her body.

Longarm held himself there for a long moment, then pressed down into her, slowly, filling her gradually, until at last he was fully inside her.

Emma moaned and wrapped her arms tight around him. She clung to him fiercely with arms and legs and greedy mouth.

He gave her time for her body to adjust to his presence there, then began to stroke in and out.

She rode the waves of sensation with him, her body responding to his, until she was pumping and bucking beneath him with a ferocious joy.

Longarm held himself back, giving her time to reach the peak. Only when he felt her responses in hard, convulsive contractions and the stiffening of her slender body beneath him did he let himself go.

He threw his head back and groaned aloud, and Emma answered with a matching cry of her own as both of them reached the peak and tumbled over it into the valley of lassitude that lay on the other side.

Longarm collapsed onto her, and she accepted his weight gladly, clinging to him and holding him there even when he tried to roll off her. She was crying softly now, but from pleasure, from joy.

After a time Longarm smiled and raised his head so that he could look into her bright green eyes. He kissed her, and she hugged him to her all the closer.

Her eyes were soft and languid as she savored the pleasures he had given her.

Then those emerald eyes widened with happy disbelief as she felt the return of his desire still inside her.

"Again?" she asked.

"Disappointed?"

Her laughing answer was not one of disappointment.

Longarm sipped the brandy she had given him. She had raided her uncle's liquor cabinet and was joining him in the daring drink.

He took her hand and squeezed it lightly, then leaned over and kissed her.

"I know," she said. "You have to go now."

"I don't want to. I hope you know that too."

"Do you . . . do you think you can come back?"

"I'm sure of it. First chance I get." He winked at her. "Until then, maybe you could do some thinking. Cobble up some story that would satisfy your aunt and uncle. You could come down and spend a weekend with me in Denver, maybe. I should have some free time next weekend."

She pressed her face into the hollow of his shoulder and nuzzled him happily. "I'll think of something. I promise."

"Good." He drained off the last of the brandy. "You're sure about those directions?"

"Oh, yes." She laughed. "Uncle Howard was *so* embarrassed when Aunt Wilda pointed it out to me. She said whatever I did when I was out for a canter or a drive, I must never *ever* stop at that house, because the lady of the house was no lady at all." She giggled and placed her hand on Longarm's thigh. "If only they knew," she said.

"Knew?"

"If only they knew how much *fun* it can be." She laughed again.

"You don't think they do?"

"Of course not, silly. They're *old!*" she said, as if that explained everything. She made a face and added, "I can't *imagine* them doing it."

Longarm smiled. Her comments made him feel rather old himself, but he understood. "What about your parents?"

"Custis. Really! Don't be *absurd.*"

It was his turn to laugh. Someday, probably soon, it would finally occur to her that her staid and straitlaced parents surely *must* have engaged in these marvelous carnal activities, or she would not be here now.

But there was time enough for her to think of that, and it was something she should do on her own, without his assistance. It had, he thought, something to do with really growing up.

He laughed again and stood up. Emma rose with him and came into his arms.

"Just once more?" she pleaded.

He shook his head. "I've been here too long already. I feel bad enough about that. There's people depending on me, and I wouldn't want to let them down."

"If you have to, then. If you'll *promise* to come back."

"I promise. First chance I get."

"I'll be here. That is a promise too. No matter how long it takes, dear, I shall be here waiting for you."

She kissed him deeply, sorrowful at the parting and already hungry again.

Longarm pulled away from her and jammed the Stetson onto his head.

Emma Emry was already missing him, but the truth would likely have offended her if he had let her know. His thoughts were already miles away in the dark, clear night, centered wholly on the Widow Swann and Arlen Cooper and a pair of youngsters named Smith.

105

Before he was out the door, Longarm had as good as forgotten about Emma.

He was thinking instead about that damned Ingersoll ticking away in his vest pocket.

With the directions Emma Emry had given him, Longarm had no trouble at all finding the Widow Swann's home this time. It was only a few miles distant from the Emry place.

As he had done once already this evening, he hobbled the horse well away from the house and made a quiet approach with his Winchester held at the ready.

Close inspection showed a lamp burning in the empty kitchen and another glowing behind closed curtains in a bedroom at the back of the place.

This time there was no doubt at all about how many people were at home.

Although this time if he was making a mistake about his intrusion it was going to be doubly damned embarrassing, because there was no doubt either about what was going on on the other side of those drawn curtains.

He could hear the snuffling snorts of a man and woman locked together in pleasure, and the bedsprings of the widow's bed were loud and busy.

Perfect, Longarm thought with a wry grin. Not too many fellows thought to keep a gun or a knife in hand when they were busy bruising bellies with a lady friend.

He made the same quiet circuit of the place as he had at Emry's, then raised the sash of the bedroom window by a few inches to make sure he could clear the sill easily.

Colt in hand, he poised himself, set his legs like a pair of giant springs, and leaped through the window with a shriek.

He dove through the curtains, pulling one of them down with him, and knocked a water pitcher off the table that he had not seen in front of the damned window.

The pitcher hit the floor with a crash and a spray of water, adding to the noise and confusion of the moment.

Longarm rolled and came to his feet facing the bed, his Colt leveled and ready.

The occupants of the bed had been frozen into stunned immobility, much like a prime example of a photographer's art.

Arlen Cooper was on his knees, pimply behind pale and hairy in the lamplight. Mrs. Swann was kneeling as well, her own ample rump tucked into Cooper's front. As a participant, the activity was jolly good sport. But from a spectator's point of view, they looked silly as hell.

Arlen Cooper was a pale, thin man with lank hair and a moustache that must have interfered severely with his meals. Random speckling of hair and bright red pimples gave him a decidedly ludicrous appearance.

The Widow Swann, for all her reputation as the neighborhood hussy, was no better looking than her boy friend.

She was a meaty middle-aged female with a large, sagging belly, fat-wrinkled and very heavy thighs, and breasts that were shapelessly pendulous.

Looking at them, naked and still coupled, Longarm managed to keep his professional composure. Both of them were slack-jawed and staring, frightened half out of their wits by the unexpected intrusion and by the gaping muzzle of the Colt that was holding rock steady on the side of Arlen Cooper's temple.

"Just the way you are is fine," Longarm said calmly. He reached inside his coat for his wallet and flashed his badge so both could see.

Cooper had been pale and frightened to begin with. Now his terror deepened. His face twisted in a silent cry and his eyes squinched shut.

"Right there," Longarm warned. He moved a step forward and used the toe of his boot to hook the pair's discarded clothing back away from the bed.

The widow let her elbows relax, lowering her head so that it rested on the pillow in front of her. Cooper's arms, braced against the softly plump planes of Mrs. Swann's wide back, were trembling.

"I need to check for weapons," Longarm said, "so don't be making me nervous with any unexpected moves. I don't expect to shoot unless I have to, but anything stupid you think up would make me have to."

Cooper nodded his comprehension. The widow stayed where she was. The tall deputy took another step forward until he was standing over the couple, and used his free hand to pull the pillows off the rumpled bed. There were no hidden weapons there.

"M...m...my..."

"Take your time, Cooper. I won't shoot you for speaking."

He nodded. "My shotgun's in the corner. Over there." He jerked his head toward the front wall of the bedroom.

"All right." Longarm went to it and picked it up. It was an old weapon and poorly cared for, a single-barrel front-loader with a cracked stock that had been wrapped in rawhide for repair. He removed the percussion cap from the steel nipple under the hammer, rendering the gun as good as empty. He slipped the cap into his coat pocket and set the shotgun back where it had been.

"What about the knife, Cooper?"

"Wha...what knife?" The man was sweating now. One slippery palm slid off Mrs. Swann's back, and he half fell on top of her.

Longarm felt calm enough, in control of the situation. He was not at all startled and certainly he was not close to shooting the murderous son of a bitch by accident. But Arlen Cooper did not have to know that.

Longarm cocked the Colt, unnecessarily since the weapon was a double-action model, and thrust it forward.

Cooper cried out and bit at his underlip in expectation of the roar of a gunshot.

"About that knife?"

"Belt. On m' belt." Cooper pointed frantically toward the floor at the side of the bed.

Longarm nodded. He knelt and with one hand felt through the pile of mingled male and female clothing. Cooper's none-too-clean trousers had a large, curved skinning knife attached to them in a fringed leather sheath. Longarm wrestled the belt free of its loops and pulled the sheath off, then stood and tucked the evidence into his own waistband.

"Is this the knife you used on them?" he asked.

Cooper thought about remaining silent, but took another look into the muzzle of Longarm's Colt. He nodded.

"I don't know anything about it," Mrs. Swann said, her voice partially muffled by the mattress against which her head rested.

"Uh-huh," Longarm muttered, not believing her for a moment. No one had yet mentioned just what crime Arlen Cooper was supposed to have committed, yet the widow woman obviously knew enough about it to deny knowledge of the unspecified crime.

Longarm knelt again and felt carefully of all the articles of clothing on the floor. There were no weapons hidden there.

"One at a time. You first, Miz Swann. You can get up and get dressed. But real slow, and where I can see what you're doing. *Real* slow."

Cooper backed away from the woman, and she left the bed awkwardly to pull her dress over her head while Longarm watched. She did not bother with her underthings.

"Now you, Cooper."

The man did as he was told. The woman returned to the bed and sat on the side of it. She did not seem uncomfortable about having been seen in a compromising situation.

"Everything," Longarm said.

"What?"

"I say put everything on. You and me are fixing to take a little trip tonight. The lady can do what she wants."

He had no intention of tipping the woman to the fact that she would be a suspect for conspiracy to commit murder. That would be up to the local authorities once he had Cooper turned over to them for prosecution. Longarm had no real reason to put her in cuffs tonight. The local boys could deal with Mrs. Swann at their leisure.

Cooper swallowed hard but nodded.

"In case you're wondering," Longarm said, his voice deceptively soft and gentle, "I was there this morning. Happened by just after you left."

Cooper stopped in the middle of pulling on his trousers and gave Longarm a look with eyes that were as cold and unfeeling as the grave. He was obviously feeling somewhat more secure now that he had his drawers on, and he had had some time to think.

"Where?" he asked.

"Your house," Longarm said.

Cooper shrugged. "I ain't been there since early yesterday. I been here ever since. Ask the lady. She'll tell you."

Mrs. Swann looked at Cooper for a moment and then at Longarm. He gave her time to make up her mind. If she spoke now she would be committing herself to Cooper, and damn well putting herself in line for a conspiracy charge. He rather hoped she would speak up on the bastard's behalf.

Mrs. Swann apparently was somewhat brighter than her

110

paramour. She wanted more facts before she made the commitment. She looked Longarm in the eye, shrugged once, and never thereafter looked directly at her beau.

Longarm grunted. He still had no cause to arrest her. "Your wife was still alive when I got there, Cooper."

The man's eyes flashed. He had his mouth half open and was on the verge of arguing that possibility. Longarm could see it clear as brass in the prick's expression. He was about to make the mistake of saying that his wife *couldn't* have been alive when Longarm found her. He caught himself barely in time and clamped his jaw stubbornly shut.

"What I think I'm gonna do," Longarm said softly, "is to leave you without handcuffs. Makes it easy for you to try and make a break for it, I know, but you'll need your hands to manage your horse, won't you?" He smiled.

"No," Cooper said quickly. "I know what you want, and I won't give it to you. I won't give you any excuses, mister. Harriet, you're a witness to this. I haven't done anything wrong, and I demand that you handcuff me an' take me to the sheriff so's I can get a fair trial. I won't try and escape. You remember I said that, Harriet. I won't do it. An' you, mister, you're responsible for my safety. You got to remember that. You're a sworn officer of the law, and you're responsible."

Cooper shoved his hands forward, fists clenched and wrists held close together, waiting for the cuffs he was demanding. "You got to take care of me, mister. You got to."

He was right, of course. Longarm remembered the scene inside the miserable bastard's house this morning. The smell of the blood, the humming buzz of the flies that were drawn to it, the sheer *amount* of it, and the awful, unbelievable things that had been done to those children and to Mrs. Cooper.

111

He looked once at Harriet Swann and again, coldly, at Arlen Cooper.

But the son of a bitch was right. Longarm had him in custody and he was sworn to bring him in for a fair and impartial trial before a duly constituted court of law.

Longarm pulled a set of cuffs from his back pocket and snapped them onto Arlen Cooper's hairy wrists.

The son of a bitch would die. There was no question about that. But it would be by a hangman's thirteen-wrap knot, and not by Custis Long's hand.

"Good evening, ma'am." Longarm touched the brim of his hat toward the woman, who was likely as vile as her boy friend, and who also would make some payment to society, if Longarm had anything to say about it. Then he led Cooper out into the chill air of the night.

Chapter 10

Longarm had two choices about the direction he could take. The thing he had to do, either way, was to get Arlen Cooper into the custody of the local authorities as quickly as possible, so that he could return to concentrating on Tom and Carrie Smith's problems.

He had to reach the railroad, where he would be able to wire the sheriff's office up the line at Keenesburg. He could not remember offhand if that was the county seat, but he knew there was at least a county deputy stationed there. Longarm had met the man before and liked him.

The choices were whether he should travel northeast to Dukes Crossing or turn southeast, back down to Childs Ferry.

He opted for Childs Ferry. It was closer to Carrie Smith's place, and would let him get back onto that job that much quicker.

He shook his head as he rode. The delay caused by Cooper had thrown him all to hell and gone, and he had had no time to begin with.

At least, he reflected, it had kept him from thinking about the office back in Denver. He sighed. He was supposed to have been there for the Saturday morning working hours. He had been so damned busy he had never once given the office a thought. Billy Vail had left him in charge. Longarm hoped Henry had been able to cope with things. If not . . . well, he would have to worry about that later. Right now the time was pressing on him as it speeded toward Tom Smith's date with the hangman early Monday.

It was past ten o'clock, closer to eleven, when Longarm and his prisoner reached Childs Ferry. The town, what there was of it, was closed up tight except for the saloon, and even that was relatively quiet for a Saturday night. There were lights and the sounds of piano playing coming from inside the saloon, but there was no shouting or loud argument to be heard. No laughter either.

Longarm led Cooper's horse past the place, although he did give some thought to the partial bottle of Maryland rye that rode in his saddlebags. He had work to do, though. He settled for a cheroot instead.

He took Cooper down to the south end of town to the livery.

The old hostler was inside, in a small harness room that had been turned into living quarters by the simple expedient of furnishing it with a cot and a coal-oil lamp. The old man opened the door at Longarm's knock, and recognition came quickly into his smile.

"G'd evenin', Marshal." He looked past Longarm to the handcuffed prisoner and the two tired horses standing in the alleyway of the barn. "Looks like you and that horse've been a far piece since you was here. Worth your trouble, was it?" He was looking at Cooper, and the expression was not friendly in spite of the greeting he had just given Long.

"Well worth it," Longarm said.

The old man grunted.

"I have a favor to ask," Longarm went on.

"Trot it out then, son."

"I have to send a wire, and these horses need tending. I'll pay for my own, of course, and I suspect the county will be taking care of this man's. What I'd like to ask you, though, to save me the trouble of keeping an eye on him,

114

is whether I can nail this jasper to the wall here while I go find the railroad agent and get my wire off. Unless you have a jail here. I didn't notice one earlier."

"Didn't notice one because there ain't one," the hostler said. "Sure, you can leave him here a while, and I'll show you where to find Louis."

Louis, Longarm gathered, would be the agent he had talked with briefly at the railroad depot earlier. He thanked the old man and followed him into his living quarters with Arlen Cooper tagging sullenly along. The man had not spoken since they had left the Widow Swann's place.

The old hostler's room was still used for the storage of harness as well as for sleeping. The walls at floor and ceiling had been more or less rat-proofed by nailing flattened tin cans along the joints. Horse collars, harnesses, and lengths of trace chain were hung on pegs, covering most of the available wall space. A six-by-six-inch support post was embedded in the floor in the center of the room and ran out of sight through the ceiling, presumably up to the rafters above the hayloft overhead. The top of the post too had been faced with flattened cans in an effort to keep rats and mice out.

The hostler pointed to the post. "Nail him to that, an' he won't be going nowhere till you say so," he said.

Longarm nodded. It would take an ax or a saw to get him free once Cooper was secured there. "Could I use some of that chain?"

"Yup."

The old man produced a short length of trace chain, and Longarm unlocked one side of the cuffs Cooper was wearing. He slipped the thin steel of the cuff through a link of the chain, took a turn around the massive post, and then put the handcuff steel through the link at the other end of the chain too before he returned the cuff to Cooper's wrist.

115

Cooper was not going anywhere now.

Cooper gave his captor a look that said he wished he was not done killing for this day, but he said nothing. He used the toe of his shoe to pull a burlap-wrapped bundle over to the base of the post and sat on it, trying to make himself comfortable.

The old hostler, who had been so pleasant and friendly with Longarm, reacted at once with a snarl and a lunge.

"Get off that," he snapped. He grabbed Cooper by the shoulder and flung him aside, then took the burlap sack and hauled it over to the side of the room where Cooper would not be able to reach it again.

"Bastard," he hissed. "That's an honest man's saddle that I said I'd keep for him, and I don't want the likes o' you scratchin' it up."

Cooper glared at the old man hatefully, but again he said nothing. He crawled to the base of the post and sat on the floor with his back against the post for a rest.

"You told me this morning you didn't know this man," Longarm said.

"Don't," the hostler agreed. He glared back at Cooper. "Heard about him since, though, by damn."

"I see."

"It's true, then?"

"That kind of depends on what you've heard."

"Butchered his woman an' three kiddies is what we was told. Neighbor of his come in here and got throwin' up drunk about it. Said he'd been one of the ones as had to try and clean up after this animal."

Longarm sighed. "That's about it."

The old man screwed up his jaw and spat at Cooper. The glob of phlegm hit Cooper in the stomach. Cooper turned his head away but kept his mouth shut.

116

"Maybe it wouldn't be safe for me to leave him here," Longarm said.

The hostler frowned, but he said, "You can leave him. He'll be alive when you get back. I'll make the promise." He paused. "For you, Marshal. Not for that shit-eater."

"I'll take you at your word, then."

The hostler went outside with Longarm and pointed out the house where the railroad agent stayed, then went back to the barn and began working on the horses. Cooper was left alone in the harness room.

"I'll be back as quick as I can," Longarm said.

He walked to the house the hostler had indicated and had to knock on the door several times before a man finally opened it. Then he had to wait some more before the railroad agent was roused and had time to dress.

"Sorry," Longarm told him. "I wouldn't bother you except for an emergency."

Louis rubbed the sleep from his eyes and walked in untied shoes and a half-buttoned shirt over to the tiny depot. He opened the office and lighted a lamp, then shoved a message form across the counter to Longarm.

The message was addressed to Deputy Jay Standford, Keenesburg, Colorado, and was marked "Urgent—immediate delivery."

"What would be the quickest way Standford could get down here?" Longarm asked the agent.

The man flipped through a sheaf of special-order flimsies and said, "There's a short freight due through at 6:10, or the regular passenger southbound later on. But I wouldn't expect to see Standford get here until the passenger comes through at 9:37, if I was you."

"Why's that?"

Louis looked at him and shrugged. "Marshal, you show

117

me a badge and tell me you got to send a wire in the middle of the damned night, why, I'll send your wire. But there won't be nobody in the Keenesburg station until just before that special freight is due, same as I wouldn't normally be here until then. If you'd told me where you wanted to send your wire you might have saved me some trouble. Though, of course, I'll send it whenever you want."

Longarm sighed. "Send the son of a bitch in the morning then. I'll look for Jay about 9:30."

"You do that, Marshal." Louis put the message form into a box on his desk, got out his ring of keys, and blew out the lamp.

Longarm yawned and stretched. Since he seemed to have no choice about the matter, he would go back to the barn and get a night's sleep. There was not much else he could do until Standford arrived and took Arlen Cooper off his hands.

He thought fleetingly about going over to the saloon for a nightcap, then decided to make do with the bottle in his saddlebags.

The railroad agent, awake now, angled toward the saloon, and Longarm went back to the livery barn.

The old hostler had not accomplished much by the time Longarm got back. Each of the horses had been given a light graining and each had a full hay bunk, but the old man was just beginning to work on Longarm's mount.

"Mind if I make my bed out here for the night?" Longarm asked.

"You wouldn't be so comfortable here as you ought," the hostler said. "Better if you take a room over at the McConnacle place. They'll fix you up there."

"Thanks, but I'd best stay here. I'm responsible for him." He pointed toward the closed door behind which Arlen Cooper was chained.

The hostler looked away and spat once before he spoke. "That the way it is then?"

"What do you mean?"

The old man shrugged.

"Do you mind if I make my bed out here?" Longarm asked again.

"You do what you feel you got to."

Longarm assumed that it was a permission of sorts, and got his bedroll.

"Fork you down some fresh hay then, damn it," the old man said grudgingly.

Longarm climbed the crude vertical ladder into the loft and kicked down enough hay to make a reasonably comfortable bed, then dropped down to ground level again and assembled hay and blankets into a fair substitute for a bed. It was a sight better than many places he had had to sleep in the past.

He arranged his gear beside the bed, including the Winchester and holstered Colt, and shared a nip from his bottle of rye with the hostler before he retired, pulling his Stetson over his eyes against the glare of the lamps the old man was still working by.

"Good night."

There was a pause and finally a grunt.

It was Longarm's sense of obligation that saved him. He could not have been asleep more than a matter of a few minutes before he woke up fretting. He had forgotten to check on his prisoner before he went to sleep. The son of a bitch likely would have to go to the outhouse before they settled in for the night.

Besides, now that he was worrying about it, Longarm would not feel satisfied until he had gone back into the harness room and checked to make sure Cooper's chains were secure and the man was where he ought to be.

Longarm resigned himself to having to get up and rolled off the piled-hay bed.

As he moved he heard something whistle dully through the air, and there was a hollow impact as something solid struck his blankets where his head had been resting just half a second earlier.

Longarm threw himself backward, Colt in hand, and rolled.

He came up short, bumping into someone's bony shins, and lashed out with an elbow to drive the man off him. The elbow caught whoever it was on the meaty part of the thigh, barely missing his balls, but the miss was close enough to deliver the message, and the intruder scuttled away smartly.

Longarm came up blinking.

He was surrounded by a crowd of men he did not recognize. There must have been eighteen or twenty of them, more than the entire resident population of Childs Ferry, more than likely, and they wore grimly knitted expressions over the bandannas that covered the lower parts of their faces.

There was no sign of the old hostler or of Louis, the railroad agent. Either or both of those men could have been the ones to tell about Arlen Cooper's presence here.

He had no doubt about what was on these jaspers' minds. Lynch mob.

These would be locals and distant neighbors of the Cooper family alike.

They would have had time to learn about the viciousness of the crime by now, and they would be wanting vengeance immediately, without giving the fancy lawyers a chance to screw things up.

Longarm stood with his feet slightly spread and the Colt held level in his hand, but pointing at no one in particular.

He brushed a hank of falling hair away from his forehead and nodded to them.

"Got you a party in mind, boys?"

"Not for you, Marshal," one of them assured him. If Longarm had ever seen or talked to the fellow before, he could not tell it now behind the cover of the bandanna.

"Uh-huh." Longarm looked pointedly toward the instrument that had been intended to give him a long, deep sleep.

It was the lead-weighted butt end of a bullwhacker's whip, reversed and swung by the thick end of the lash.

A blow from a chunk like that would have put him to sleep all right, and quite possibly caved in the front of his skull as well.

"Honest," the man said, possibly guessing what Longarm was thinking.

"I got to give you credit," Longarm said. "You're a sneaky bunch. I never heard you coming." He looked more closely and saw that all of them had left their boots or shoes behind when they approached the barn. They had come barefoot on the straw-littered earth floor and had been able to make no sound. Even so, it was a sign of Longarm's fatigue that they had been able to reach him without his knowledge.

Conscious knowledge, anyway. Something had wakened him in time, but he had been too tired to realize the danger and had been thinking only of his prisoner.

Cooper. Longarm turned his head toward the harness room.

There were three of them immediately outside the room, but the door was still closed. One man stood with his hand on the knob.

That man carried a coil of hemp rope, something heavier and hairier than a cowhand's lariat. The other two had neatly coiled bullwhips in their hands.

Their intentions were clear enough. Arlen Cooper was expected to make payment the long, hard way before death finally released him from his crimes.

Longarm could understand these men's desire. But he could not permit them to fulfill it.

"Back away now, boys. This one the law'll take care of without you."

"We can't do that, Marshal," one of the masked men said. "Agatha Cooper was sister to my missus. Them kids was my niece an' nephews. They was kin, and now they're chopped meat. I can't walk away from that."

The man seemed to realize that he had as good as identified himself. He fixed Longarm with a steady stare and reached to pull his mask down around his neck where the knotted bandanna belonged.

He was a handsome man somewhere in his forties. He did not waver or look away from Longarm's penetrating gaze.

"My name is Cortland Lane," he said in a steady voice. "I live a few miles east from the Cooper place. And those was my kin that died this morning. I come here, and so did these other boys, to see that the debt is paid for what was done."

"Cooper will hang, Mr. Lane," Longarm said evenly, "but he will hang legal and proper, ordered by a court of law in the state of Colorado. I was there, you know. Your sister-in-law died in my arms this morning. She made a deathbed statement about who done the killings. I'll testify to that, and Arlen Cooper will hang."

One of the other men, still masked, snickered. "I reckon you c'n guarantee that, Marshal?"

"As good as."

"Don't be giving us no bullshit, Marshal. We see the shit

122

that happens in those city courtrooms. We're country folk, but we ain't a bunch of ignorant rubes. We get the city papers out here. We c'n read. We know what c'n happen to the truth once you get a bunch of city fellers to poking it with sharp pencils."

"I'm not giving you any bull," Longarm said. "I've seen the inside of more courtrooms than any of you has seen shithouses, and I'm telling you Arlen Cooper will hang."

"But you can't guarantee it," Lane said.

"Of course I can't *guarantee* it. It isn't my place to be the judge or the jury. Nor your place either. That's what the laws are for. The law will take care of Cooper."

"Or not. Dependin'," the masked man said.

"We're serious about this, Marshal. Justice got to be done here. We don't give a shit about law. We're interested in justice."

Another man and then another stripped the masks away from their faces until all but two of them stood boldly exposed for Longarm's identification if it came to that.

This was no mob of temporarily irate drunks, Longarm realized. These were good, honest men who were filled with a coldly righteous anger.

They wanted justice, and they had no real confidence that the law would provide it.

Longarm wished they would go the hell away. He was duty bound to protect Arlen Cooper and bring the bastard in for trial. He did not want to arrest any of these men; much less would he want to have to kill any of them.

He would feel no regret or hesitation whatsoever if a mob of drunken assholes came and tried to take a prisoner of his. In a situation like that the solution was simple. Pick one. Any one would do, but the leader was best. Lay it on him hard and clean with the threat or, if required, the reality of a slug from the big .44. And then ask who wanted to be the next man to die.

Tactics like that were enough to sober up the most thoroughly sauced jehu.

But these men were not drunk. They were not some roaring, weaving mob. They were righteous. And in many ways Longarm had to admit they were right. There were no guarantees in a court of law. There could not be, or the system would not be an honest one.

He could explain all this, and these men would listen. They were that kind, he believed, or they would never have had the courage to remove their masks.

But, damn it, they already knew all of the arguments Longarm might propose. They knew them already, and had rejected them.

Longarm grimaced and moved through the crowd to the closed door. The men who had been about to enter backed away from it to give him room. None of them tried to club him from behind, as he had more than half expected.

He stood with his back against the door and the Colt in his fist.

"I won't try to persuade you," he said. "You've thought this over and talked it over, and I won't insult your intelligence by thinking I can come up with anything you haven't already considered."

Several of the men nodded.

"What I will say is this," Longarm said. "My sworn duty is to deliver Arlen Cooper to the law. You boys feel yours is something different. Yesterday or tomorrow, either one, I'd be proud to share a drink with any or all of you. But until Cooper is delivered to your sheriff all legal and signed for, I'm responsible for him. Until then I got to oppose you." He smiled grimly and reached for a cheroot before he realized that the thin cigars were in his coat, and that was still folded and laid beside his bed.

"Something you want, Marshal?" one of the men asked.

"Toss me that coat, would you, please?"

One of them did. He shoved the Colt behind his waistband, took out a cheroot, and lighted it. "Thanks. I'd offer them, but I don't have enough to go around."

"That's all right, Marshal."

Longarm nodded. "The choices are clear, boys, even if they aren't pleasant. I got to stand against you tonight. I'm not damn fool enough to tell you that you can't take Cooper from me. If you're willing to shoot me down or burn me out, well, it's me against the whole lot of you. I don't expect I'd come out of it alive, and I don't expect many of you would either. But you could get 'er done if you're that determined on it." He drew on the cheroot for a moment until the coal at the tip glowed brightly, then held it away for a second to admire it. The smoke tasted good. A drink to go with it would have been even better.

"The thing is, boys," he said calmly, "I got to stand here against you, come what may. I don't especially want to shoot any of you, and I sure don't want to be shot by you. But that's the way it will have to be if you press it." He smiled at Lane and then at the others. "The choice is yours now, boys."

The men looked at Longarm and at each other. Very few of them carried guns. Mostly they were armed with ropes or whips or cudgels. One man carried a shotgun and several others wore everyday revolvers belted at their waists, but none of them had come out in search of a gunfight.

Longarm leaned back against the door, smoking his cheroot and waiting.

There was a stir of uncertainty among the men. They

moved quietly about in the lamplight, whispering softly among themselves.

After half a minute or less, Cort Lane moved forward. "We'll talk it over some more, Marshal, and let you know."

"All right."

"One thing I can tell you now, Marshal."

"Yes, Lane?"

"If we come against you, we'll give fair warning of it. You won't be shot down outa the night."

Longarm looked into the man's eyes and saw the truth there. They had been willing to slip up on him and knock him senseless. They would have considered that to be a fair play. But these men were not assassins who would shoot from ambush. If they came again, they would do it the way they thought was right.

"All right, Lane. I couldn't ask for fairer."

Lane smiled at him. "I'll see you later, Marshal."

Longarm raised an eyebrow, thinking that Lane, at least, had already reached his decision, and that it was not the one Longarm would have hoped for.

Lane chuckled. "What I meant, Marshal, was that I'll see you again tonight, or else somewhere down the line. If there's a trial you can be sure I'll be there."

"If you come again tonight, I reckon I can be sure you'd be there too, Lane."

"You can for a fact, Marshal."

Longarm held his hand out, and Lane shook it.

"I won't wish you luck, Lane."

"Then wish me justice."

"That I do, man. Every day of my life."

Lane nodded, and the men filed out into the darkness that surrounded the barn.

Longarm went back to his bed, but not to sleep again.

He pulled his boots on and buckled his gunbelt in place, picked up his saddlebags and Winchester, and went back to the door that shielded Arlen Cooper.

He sat on the floor with his back to the door and reached into the saddlebags for what was left of the bottle of rye.

There was nothing he could do now but wait.

Chapter 11

An hour passed and they had not returned. That did not necessarily mean that they would not return, only that they had not.

Longarm stood and stretched. If Lane and the other reasonable men like him were going to come, they likely would have by now. But there could be others in the same town filled with drink and with anger who would decide at some point during the night that the rules laid down by Lane and his kind should now be changed. That there was nothing so wrong about disposing of some deputy marshal in the name of a good cause.

Longarm went over to the horses, still in the tie-stalls where the hostler had left them, and made sure the animals could reach the hay the old man had put out for them. Longarm had seen no sign of the hostler since he went to sleep. Apparently the old fellow had known what was coming and had chosen to meet the issue by simply avoiding it. In a way, Longarm could not blame him.

He blew out the lamps the hostler had been using, plunging the barn into darkness.

If anyone came now, apart from Cort Lane and his promises, there was all too good a chance that the next bunch might want a bullet to clear the path for them. If so, there was no sense in making it easy for them.

A thread of yellow light showed under the door to the harness room. There was no point in burning that either.

Longarm opened the door and went inside to his prisoner.

He got a surprise when he looked at Cooper. Someone, almost certainly the hostler, although it could have been another, had paid the man a visit earlier.

The side of Cooper's face was a raw purple and red bruise, and his lower lip was split and puffy. His left eye was mostly closed. It looked like someone had kicked him.

"You're supposed to protect me," Cooper said sullenly.

"If you aren't deaf, you already heard that I've been doing that."

"You call this protection?"

"You're breathing." In truth, Longarm was not able to work up a whole hell of a lot of sympathy for a man who would do what Arlen Cooper had done.

As a deputy United States marshal, Long was pledged to deliver a live Cooper to Jay Standford come morning. As a man, it did not hurt his feelings at all to see Cooper's current state. If it had not been for the badge in his coat pocket, Longarm would likely be interested in doing some rough and immediate justice himself.

"But—"

"Shut your mouth and do what you're told. Or make a break for it if you'd rather. At least then I could get a night's sleep instead of having to worry about the likes of you."

Cooper shut up and did what he was told.

Longarm unchained him from the post in the harness room, where the townsmen knew him to be, blew the lamp out, and took Cooper out into the barn.

He led him into one of the unoccupied box stalls and chained him to the support post between it and the neighboring stall.

"It stinks in here," Cooper mumbled.

"Uh-huh, but the air will clear as soon as you're gone," Longarm said.

Cooper shut up again.

"You do whatever you've a mind to, but if it was me I think I'd set down in the corner and make like I wasn't here. Folks don't like you very much, Cooper. Neither do I."

The rattle of chains in the darkness told Longarm that he was being obeyed. Longarm went back to his vigil in front of the now empty harness room.

Another hour passed, and a third.

Longarm's eyes felt gritty and painful from lack of sleep and frequent rubbing, but there was no help for it. He had to stay awake or risk losing his prisoner—or worse.

"You still there?" Cooper asked from time to time in a frightened whisper.

"I'm here," Longarm assured him.

Once, along about four or four-thirty, Cooper screamed.

Longarm came to his feet in a lurch, the muzzle of his Colt searching for a target he could not see.

Cooper was in tears, babbling something Longarm could not understand.

The sound, though, proved that he was still alive.

"What is it?" There was no immediate answer, only the sounds of Cooper crying. "What is it, damn it?"

"Rats," Cooper whimpered. "I can't stand rats."

Longarm grunted and sat down again. There were things he had to protect Cooper from. He did not figure that rats were in that category.

Dawn brought with it the sound of boot heels crunching on the gravel outside the barn. One man, making no attempt to hide his approach. Longarm stood, yawning. The old hostler was finally coming home from wherever he had spent the night, Longarm thought.

The sound of the footsteps came from the side of the barn, toward the open sliding doors at the front.

They stopped beside the thin planking of the wall just outside the harness room, and Longarm heard the sound of oiled metal as a pair of hammers were drawn back.

He jumped for the front of the barn, but too late. One bellowing scattergun blast followed another as a pair of heavy charges were sent into and through the wall, aimed inside the harness room to the place where Cooper had been chained earlier.

Longarm threw himself through the doorway.

The gunman had already dropped the empty shotgun and was aiming a long-barreled cap-and-ball pistol toward the doorway where Longarm now was. There was not enough light to see clearly who the shooter was.

Longarm hit the ground rolling, and the gunman tracked him with the absolutely immense muzzle of the old horse pistol.

Longarm fired first, his Colt rocking in his fist and a thin spread of white smoke rising between himself and the man with the pistol.

Longarm's first bullet struck the man on the point of his hip, and the impact turned him to the side.

His finger squeezed involuntarily on the trigger, and the old gun fired with a roar and a broad sheet of yellow flame.

The thing had been loaded with buck and ball, a multiple charge of one large ball and a number of smaller ones.

Dirt and chips of sharp gravel sprayed into Longarm's face as the spreading charge splattered the ground in front of him. One pellet, thankfully no larger than a No. 2 shot, sliced down his back from shoulder blade to waist until it struck his belt and ricochetted off somewhere.

Longarm fired again. It did not occur to him until a moment afterward that there was no need for him to shoot again. Both the shotgun and the pistol had to be empty now. The man could not have tried for him again. But by the

132

time he realized that, it was too late. A soft lead slug from his Colt had already ripped the gunman's throat out, and the man was on the ground face forward with his lifeblood spilling into the dirt, and his legs beating a rapid tattoo of death on the hard ground.

"Jesus." Longarm came to his knees and then shakily to his feet.

His back was sticky with seeping blood from the split skin where the pellet had passed. He tried to reach it to assess the extent of the injury but could not.

Someone came running from the direction of the saloon. There were a good many others running behind him.

Longarm turned his Colt on them and ordered them to halt. They did, at once. Longarm was in no mood for games now. He would have shot and likely they could see that in the set of his jaw and the cold fire that was in his eyes.

Cort Lane, Longarm saw, was not among them, although he recognized most of the crowd from the visit they had paid earlier.

One of the men, who wore no gunbelt and who at the moment was bareheaded and empty-handed, disengaged himself from the group and came a little closer.

"This wasn't what we'd decided on," he said. "We talked it over, and this wasn't what the rest of us decided to do here."

Longarm nodded.

"Cort had promised we'd tell you if we came. We would have."

"And this man?" Longarm gestured toward the body with the Colt.

"That's Cort's brother, Reston Lane," the man said.

"He's restin' now," some wag in the crowd snickered. Longarm guessed that that one had spent the night doing some drinking.

"This past day or so hasn't been much for the Lane family," Longarm said wearily. He felt more tired than he could remember feeling in a very long time, and the blood that was still clotting on his back was not helping any. "Well, it hasn't been a pleasure for me either. I reckon you can take his brother to him now, with my apologies."

The spokesman nodded, and several men came forward to pick up Reston Lane's body and carry it off toward a group of wagons parked in front of the saloon.

"I can't speak for Cort, you know," the spokesman said apologetically.

"I know."

"He might want to . . . well . . ."

"I know. I'll be here if he feels that way about it."

"I know the man well enough to tell you one thing, Marshal. If he comes, it'll be face to face."

"I figured." Longarm wished they would go away. He wished he could have a long drink and a hot bath and a good twenty-four hours of sleep.

But none of that was possible. And it was very likely that Cortland Lane would be on his way back to town soon, with a gun in his hand.

There were times, albeit rare ones, when Custis Long thought life might have been simpler if he had chosen to become a clerk in a ladies' haberdashery or some such, instead of pinning on a badge.

It was not that he was afraid of Lane, or any of them. Or, for that matter, all of them.

It was just that he was so damned *tired*.

And there was very little time left before Tom Smith, Jr. would die and Carrie Smith's life would collapse around her.

He holstered the Colt and walked slowly back inside the

barn while the group of townsmen accompanied Reston Lane's body to the wagons.

Arlen Cooper was safe and secure in the stall where Longarm had chained him. He was terror-stricken and tear-streaked and had a yellowish scum of fresh vomit stinking up the front of his trousers.

Longarm resisted an urge to kick the son of a bitch and went back to waiting for Jay Standford to arrive from Keenesburg.

Longarm swayed and tottered. His face was pale, a striking contrast with the brown sweep of his moustache and the healthy gloss of his hair.

Deputy Sheriff Jay Standford, a short, heavily muscled ball of fire who was as straight a peace officer as any Longarm had ever met, accepted Longarm's handcuff keys and transferred Arlen Cooper into his own set of cuffs.

"Do you want me to give you a receipt for the prisoner, Longarm?"

"Yeah, I . . ." Longarm felt fuzzy-headed and light. So light that he felt he was floating. Floating softly. It felt so very nice. So very . . .

There was the smell of earth and manure in his nose, and something was obstructing his vision.

The dirt floor of the barn.

Funny. He did not remember lying down. So how had he gotten there?

"You. Help me with him." It was Jay's voice. Longarm recognized it. But it sounded distant and sort of hollow.

"He's passed out," Jay was saying. "Son of a bitch, man. His back's all covered with blood. Jesus. How long's he been standing guard like this? Never mind. Help me get him to the doctor."

"No sawbones in this town." The voice was that of the old hostler. Longarm recognized it too although the old man, like Jay, was talking now like he was at the bottom of a well or something. The sounds were distorted. It was odd.

"Isn't there someplace . . . ?"

"You . . . you can take him to my place." The voice was that of a woman. Longarm thought he might have heard it before, but he could not remember where or when.

Jay's voice again. "All right. Help me move hi . . ."

It was the last thing Longarm remembered. A dark, red-gray fuzz closed in around him, and he floated off to a pleasant, peaceable place that had no ties to the rest of the world he had always known.

He moved slowly, wincing. He was in a bedroom. The shades had been drawn down over the windows, and he had no idea how long he had been out, although he could see that there was daylight beyond the roller shades.

An agony unconnected with the pain in his back brought him upright into a sitting position.

Smith. The boy had been set to die on the hangman's gallows this morning. If it was daylight outside, Longarm had failed him and his sister.

The fleeing time had finally run its course. He groaned and cried out aloud.

"What is it?"

The girl rushed to the bedroom door at the sound of Longarm's voice.

Seeing her, recognizing and remembering, gave him at least some idea of where he had to be. He was still in Childs Ferry.

The girl who was watching over him was the plain, mousy girl who had been waiting tables at the cafe where he had had the late breakfast on Saturday, the one who had been so pleased when he complimented her.

"It's . . . nothing," Longarm said. Nothing worth talking about, anyway. It was too late now for it to matter. By now Tom Smith, Jr. was already dead. And his little sister was a child who was as good as a whore already. There was little Longarm could do about that now.

Little but perhaps not exactly nothing. He could try to find the child a job. Something, he did not know what. He had not been able to save her brother. Perhaps he could still save the sister.

"You aren't in pain?" the waitress asked.

Longarm shook his head. He looked down at himself. His entire torso had been wrapped with strips of bleached linen. Aside from that, he seemed to be naked under the thin sheet that covered him. He pulled the sheet higher.

"Let me help you," the girl said. She came to the side of the bed and arranged several pillows behind him, plumping them and fluffing them until she was satisfied. Then she put a strong hand high on his back, just below the nape of his neck, and helped ease him back against the pillows. "Is that all right?"

"Fine. Thank you." He looked at her.

Oddly, she blushed and turned her eyes away from his.

"I don't even know your name," Longarm said.

She blushed again, furiously bright. "Saundra," she said. "Saundra Crowe."

"My pleasure, Miss Crowe. I'm—"

"I know," she said quickly. "Deputy Standford told me about you when he brought you over here. You're Mr. Long, a federal deputy out of Denver. He told me."

"Longarm to my friends, though. If it wouldn't make you uncomfortable to use a nickname for a strange man who's invaded your home. You're very kind to've helped me, Saundra. Thank you."

Another blush. Then, remembering something, she snapped her fingers and dashed out of the room. She returned a moment later with a piece of paper.

"Deputy Standford left this for you."

"Thanks." It was the receipt Jay had promised to give for the prisoner, jotted out on a telegraph message form from the depot.

"Did Jay get the prisoner safely away, then?"

"Oh, yes. Out on the afternoon northbound. He said you could send him a depo . . . depo-something or other."

"Deposition?" Longarm prompted.

"That was it. He said you could send him one of those when you felt up to it, and he'll get in touch with you later about the, uh, pros . . . prosecution." She looked worried. "Was that right?"

"Exactly right," he assured her.

She snapped her fingers and once again dashed away from the room. This time she returned with a tray bearing a bowl of steaming soup and a large spoon. There was a glass of milk, too, which she insisted he drink. Then she insisted on feeding him the soup.

Longarm gave in to her. It seemed easier than argument. At the moment, thinking about the dead youngster named Smith, he did not feel up to arguing about anything so damned trivial as a bowl of soup.

"You lost an awful lot of blood," Saundra explained as she raised one careful spoonful after another to his lips. "Deputy Standford said I should fill you up on soup and milk to build your blood back. Mr. Morris said I should give you red meat instead. Soon as you finish this soup I'll see can I find you some meat."

"Who's Mr. Morris?"

"From the livery. You know."

"Oh." It was the first time he had heard the old man's name.

"Anyway, you really did lose a lot of blood. That's why you went down like you did." She frowned. "The whole town'd been watching you for hours, wondering when you were going to fall down. You looked like you should've just ages ago. But you didn't. Not until Deputy Standford got there. I think some of the men, well, I think some of them had some devilment in mind if you did pass out."

She turned her head away in shame. "I should've done something to help you. But I didn't. I knew they'd be awful mad at me if I did and . . . I just didn't have the courage to do what I knew was right. I hope you'll accept my apology?"

"None necessary," Longarm said. "This is your town. I wouldn't want you to start anything against the people here."

"It's . . . it wasn't right, watching like that and not helping . . . but it's just that this house that Mama and Daddy left me, and my job at the cafe, that's all I got, Mr. Long. I'm sorry, though. I should've done better by you."

"No," he said, "you've done more than I could have asked of you. And I thank you."

"Thank you for bein' such a gentleman about it." She sighed. "I don't see many real gentlemen around here."

Longarm laughed. "There are plenty who would disagree that you've seen one yet, miss."

"Saundra."

"Only if you drop the 'mister' from my name."

She gave him a shy smile. "Okay."

Longarm looked around the room. It was small but tidy and very clean. "My gunbelt . . ."

"Out in the parlor," she said. "They brought all your things over after they'd got you into the bed."

"Did they, uh . . . ?" He waved his hand over the general

139

vicinity of his lap. He was quite naked except for the sheet and the bandages.

Saundra blushed again, brighter than ever.

"I see," he said. He damn sure had no secrets from her.

"I washed your things," she said quickly. "They wouldn't've been worth burning if I didn't."

"Would you mind bringing my gunbelt, Saundra? And maybe the bottle that's in my saddlebags? I think a nip of rye is just the thing for building new blood."

She seemed glad of the change of subject and ran lightly out of the room, to return moments later with his holstered Colt and saddlebags.

She brought a glass for him while he pulled the jug of Maryland rye, nearly empty now, from the saddlebags. Lord, but he was weak. It was a trial just getting the buckles free so he could get at the bottle. Saundra helped him with the stubborn cork and poured the liquor for him. He was able to manage the glass by himself.

"I should have asked first," he said when the good whiskey was spreading its warmth through his stomach. "I hope I haven't offended you by drinking under your roof."

"No. Not at all," she said quickly.

Longarm nodded and smiled. There were things he wanted to say to her, things he wanted to ask. But the combined effects of the hot soup and the excellent rye were pulling at him, drawing him downward toward a gentle place. His head lolled back against the pillows she had set behind him, and his eyelids closed.

Later. He could ask her things later.

He went away again.

And this time, for the first time since he had walked out of Billy Vail's office with Carrie Smith at his side, the unheard but inexorable ticking of the Ingersoll was not weighing on him.

140

It was already too late for that.

And the truth was that his lapse into sleep again was as much an escape from that knowledge as it was a need for recuperation.

Custis Long had failed, and Tom Smith, Jr. was dead. There was just no way to change that now.

Chapter 12

He woke again with a certainty that he was not alone in the room, although he sensed no danger. He came awake without movement, sure that he had not slept long this time, and barely opened one eye.

The girl Saundra was standing near the bed. Her hands were empty, so she had not come in to feed him again. She seemed only to be looking at him.

It was curious, he thought. And so was the direction she was staring. Down toward...

Then he realized. While he slept the sheet had worked itself down below his waist.

She was looking at him there. She looked to be... he had to search for it a moment before he realized. She looked sad.

Covertly he watched her watching him.

She was a plain girl. That was the very best and most charitable way he could put it. As drab as a mouse in hair and complexion alike. If she had a figure at all, it was well hidden under the shapeless dress that hung from her thin shoulders and found no curves to cling to on its way to the floor.

She was not the sort of girl who would ever be the recipient of a gentleman's flattery, which was exactly why he had chosen to compliment her before. The treat had been a rare and pleasing one to her, as he had hoped.

Likely she would never receive another. And one day

she would end up married to a dry-land farmer who needed a chore hand and a night-time convenience, and so would consent to take her into his home.

Longarm felt sorry for her, for the life she was living now and more for the life she would inevitably have in the future, but grateful to her as well for the kindnesses she had shown him.

It was not gratitude, though, but her undisguised longing that brought a perfectly normal and natural response into his groin and began slowly to cause his shaft to lengthen and grow thicker under her wistful gaze.

He realized it, could not stop it, and began to feel a quick flush of heat in his cheeks.

"Oh!"

Her hand flew to her mouth in surprise, and Saundra looked at his open eyes. "You ... you're ..." She turned and would have fled, but he stopped her with a word.

"Wait."

Quickly he covered himself, but by then it was much too late to hide the erection that held the sheet away from his body like a tent pole.

"I'm sorry," he said. "I've embarrassed you. It's a poor way to repay you."

Saundra's plain face twisted, and shiny tear tracks streaked her face as the salty droplets ran down toward her chin. She came to the side of the bed and knelt beside him there, one hand soft on his upper arm.

"You're such a fine, handsome gentleman. I know I shouldn't have peeked, but I couldn't help myself."

"It's all right. It's all right, Saundra."

"No. It isn't. It will never be all right. I'll never be pretty enough to have a fine gentleman like you look at me. Not the way a man should look at a woman."

Longarm cupped her chin in his palm and drew her face

closer to his. She offered no resistance and seemed not at all frightened. He approached her the way he would have a skittish colt. If she wanted to run, she could. He would not try to hold her. But if she wished to stay...

He kissed her. She was nothing to look at, but her breath was sweet and the taste of her was nice. A tear tickled the corner of his mouth where his lips met hers. He brushed it away from both their faces and kissed her again.

Saundra sighed. She took his hand and moved it down to her breast.

There was little enough there to feel. A small, soft rise on the hard plane of her chest, no thicker than a saucer inverted on the top of a table. Yet soft and warmly yielding to his touch.

He found her nipple behind the covering of cloth and rolled it lightly between his thumb and forefinger. Saundra moaned and moved closer to him.

"Would you? Please? I'll beg you if I have to," she whispered. "I got no pride about it, Mr. Long. You're the finest, handsomest man I'll ever know, and if that's what it takes, well, I'll be begging you now."

Longarm kissed her again and fondled her gently. "You're a lovely young woman, Saundra Crowe," he lied, "and I would be honored to be with you."

She backed off and cried for a moment, but only for a moment. She dried her tears on the backs of her work-roughened hands and quickly stripped off the drab house-dress.

She wore little under it. Loose cotton drawers that tied at the waist, a utilitarian garment that was hardly feminine or enticing. A thin camisole. Heavy shoes but no stockings. She pulled them off and stood before him, naked, head turned away, obviously afraid of how he might react to the sight of her body.

145

She was painfully thin, he saw; the slightness of her meager breasts was in complete proportion to the rest of her frail body. Even her thighs were not meaty, and her pelvic bones were sharply prominent on either side of an inward-curving belly.

Longarm smiled at her. "You're lovely."

With a glad cry she scrambled onto the bed beside him and began covering him with moist, frantic kisses.

Longarm chuckled and drew her up so that they lay face to face. He kissed her again, deep and thorough, and gave her time to grow calm within his embrace.

Saundra sighed and snuggled happily against his chest, enjoying his kisses and the feel of his hands light but knowing on her skin.

Once she sat up, pulling away from him with a stricken look on her face.

"What is it?"

"You're hurt. I shouldn't be bothering you."

He laughed. "It's my back that's hurt, and you aren't *bothering* me at all. Except in the very nicest kind of way."

"You're sure?"

"Absolutely." He pulled her down to him again. She was hesitant for a while, then bolder.

She moved and wriggled and touched, kissing him for a while, then changing position so she could see. She seemed to want to learn every shape and texture and flavor of him.

Her hands moved over him as if they had a separate existence from the rest of her body.

She touched and lifted and held him, running her hands over every part of him she could reach and appearing to regret that she could not touch more of him because of the bandages that were in her way.

She leaned close and rubbed his flesh with the tip of her nose, drinking in the scents of his male body.

146

She kissed him everywhere she could reach as well and surreptitiously, as if she were doing something she should not be, tasted of him too.

"It's all right if you want to do that," he said at one point.

"Is it? Truly?"

"Of course. Here, let me show you."

He pulled her around until they lay side by side again, but with her head to his crotch and vice versa. "Now," he said. "You explore and play all you want down there, and I'll do the same here."

He leaned forward. Saundra blushed, but she opened herself to him. She was fresh and sweet, and he patiently gave her the sensations that had been lacking.

Saundra quivered and cried out several times. She lay with her eyes closed, giving herself completely to the feelings he brought boiling through her veins.

After a very little while she tensed and shuddered.

Longarm kissed her there and relaxed.

"Oh, I . . . I forgot."

"Forgot what?"

"I forgot . . . what I wanted to do. To you, I mean. It's just that it was so awful nice that I forgot I should be doing for you too."

"No hurry," he said amiably. "One at a time is just fine."

She bent to him, tracing his length with the tip of her tongue, savoring him, taking him into her mouth little by little. She probably could feel his growing arousal as he tipped toward the brink. In the midst of pleasing him she pulled away and asked, "Could I ask you something awful dumb?"

"It ain't dumb if you don't know the answer," he said.

She blushed. "Somebody told me once that a girl couldn't get, you know, in the family way, if she pleased a man here."

"That's true," he said.

"Then would you mind awfully if you finish this way instead of the other? I just couldn't bear to have a child and be all alone."

He stroked the side of her face and let his hand rove lightly down over her tiny swell of breast and across her bony hip. She shivered with pleasure at his touch. "I want you to be comfortable and happy," he said honestly. "Whatever way you want is fine by me."

She went back to him, more comfortable with it now. She obviously knew little about the acts of sex and had experienced even less, yet she was eager and willing, and seemed to be enjoying it quite as much as he did.

Which was, he admitted to himself, considerable.

"You're terrific," he assured her.

"Show me then."

She went back to him, pulling him deeper and harder into her mouth now, and quickly the warm rise began again deep inside his groin, flowing with an ever-increasing pressure until he could contain it no longer, and he burst out in a strong, pulsing flow into her.

"Do you think we could do that again? If you're feeling up to it, that is," she said.

Longarm laughed, and Saundra colored. "I didn't mean it *that* way, you know."

"I know."

"Well? Can we?"

Longarm laughed and kissed her navel. "Yes. We certainly can. As many times as I'm able and as many times as you like."

Saundra smiled and laid her head down on him, pressing her cheek against his belly and sighing deeply.

She was a greedy little thing, though. Even while she

gave him a few minutes to rest, her fingers continued to explore him and her hands were busy.

Her hips writhed slowly with the anticipation of pleasures yet to come, and every few seconds she would break into a broad, satisfied smile.

Chapter 13

Longarm watched with a slow, languid pleasure as Saundra left the bed and pulled her clothes on. It was coming on toward evening, and he felt good. Weak and still tired but good, everything considered. He still had regrets, many of them. But it was not his way to grieve over things he could no longer change.

In addition to the sense of failure about Tom Smith, Jr., though, he felt no small degree of concern about what was going to happen when he got back to the office. Not only had he taken Friday afternoon and Saturday morning away from his duties, now he had gone and missed the whole of Monday as well, because it was gathering toward dusk beyond the closed shades of Saundra's bedroom window.

Billy was going to snort and raise hell when he got back. At the very least he was in for a chewing over the likes of which he had not had since he was a pup.

There was no help for it now, though. The damages had been done already and could not be called back. And he truly was still mighty weak. It was unlike him to take so long to recuperate from a simple loss of blood, but it was a fact. He chalked it up to a matter of aging and reached for a cheroot while Saundra bent over and pulled the hem of her dress high so she could get at the laces of her shoes.

He smiled at her. After the highly enjoyable time they had spent together in this bed, the girl was no prettier than before, but he no longer noticed. Now she was not just some plain, homely girl who waited tables in a plain, homely town. Now she was Saundra, a person who cared for him and for whom he cared in his own quiet way, and never again would be able to see her as she appeared on the surface, only as she was inside. And inside, her heart and mind were generous and giving and sweet. He smiled at her with real affection.

"Where are you off to?" he asked and scraped a match aflame to light the cheroot.

"Mr. Morris said you need red meat, so I thought I'd go over to the cafe and get you a steak. You need something solid now to build you up again."

He nodded and once again reached for his clothes. "Get two, then. One for each of us." He smiled. "My treat, if you'll do me the honor of dining with me."

The wording pleased her. She seemed to have gotten over her habit of blushing nearly every time he spoke to her, but her pleasure and appreciation were no less genuine than they had been. She positively glowed from the slightest compliment or pleasant turn of phrase. When she smiled he noticed for the first time that she had tiny dimples in her cheeks.

Longarm fished a tiny five-dollar half-eagle out of his pocket and gave it to her. It was enough to buy more steaks than this frail girl could carry in one trip.

He thought about asking her to buy a bottle of rye whiskey as well, then rejected the request. It probably would make her feel awkward at best to be seen purchasing hard liquor for a man who was known to be under her roof. Worse, it could be compromising for her as well. He decided to let that go. Soon enough he would feel up to getting out and around, and then he could buy his own belly-warmer.

"What do you like with your steak?" she asked.

"Taters fried in grease, just like I prefer the meat done."

"Nothing else?"

He shook his head.

Saundra bent and kissed him fondly, and rather deeply as well for a trip that should take only minutes. In fact, if she had kept on much longer with the goodbye kiss, there would have been no goodbye.

"Would you like something to read while I'm gone?"

"Sure."

She stopped to find a none-too-new copy of the *Denver Post* and tossed it onto the bed beside him, blew him one last kiss, and left the house. He could hear her heels tapping light and quick on the hardwood flooring. He smiled and opened the newspaper.

He chuckled to himself. The latest Saundra had in her home seemed to be last Monday's newspaper. He grinned and settled back against the pillows she had propped behind him, the cheroot stuck at a jaunty angle in the corner of his jaw. What the hell, he had read the paper before but it had been long enough ago for him to forget most of what was in it. That was practically as good as it being fresh news.

Saundra returned home laughing, with a slightly bloody and definitely large package in one hand and a small poke of potatoes in the other. She deposited the food in the kitchen, stoked the coal fire in the stove, and went into the bedroom to give Longarm a hello kiss. She was still chuckling.

"What's so funny?" he asked.

"Oh, Mr. Morris. He's been on my mind today anyway." She smiled. "Because of you, of course." She flounced onto the side of the bed and gave him another, more serious kiss.

"And?"

"You wouldn't know, I suppose, not being from around here, but Mr. Morris must be terribly rich. Everyone thinks so. Because he is the tightest man with a penny you've ever

153

seen." She bent and began to unlace her shoes. Obviously she had some plans for after supper was over. Or before. Or both.

"Yes?" It still did not sound particularly amusing.

"Oh, it's just him. He's so tight he's cute, almost. Janie was telling me that he was in the cafe for supper this evening. It's his one big treat every week, and he was grumbling about all the money he's been losing on a board bill. As if he couldn't afford it. Gee." She shook her head in wonder. "Something about these horses being left for a week now and the owners were supposed to be back in a few days, and now he's worried he'll be stuck for the board bill. Janie said he was grumbling about not thinking in time to talk to Deputy Standford about it when he was here this morning. About how long it would have to be before he could attach the horses and get title to them or— What's wrong?"

"Wrong?"

"You have this funny expression. Like I said something I shouldn't have."

"Did you just say that Jay Standford was here this morning?"

"Sure. My gosh, surely you remember *that*. You turned that man over to him, and he gave you the receipt, and . . . Where are you going?"

Longarm was out of the bed, weak and wobbly but on his feet, and already pulling on clothing with frantic speed.

"Did I say something wrong?" Saundra sounded almost frightened.

He whirled and grabbed her by the shoulders, pulling her to him and giving her a loud, smacking kiss. "Wrong? Absolutely *not*. You said something just right, and I thank you for it. And there are some other people who might be thanking you as well. In fact, girl, you might just have saved a nice young man's life."

154

Saundra looked confused. She sat with her jaw agape while Longarm hurriedly finished dressing, strapped on his Colt, and headed over to the livery barn.

He left his gear behind. There was not all that much to it, but he quite honestly did not feel strong enough to be toting it around with him right now.

And it looked like he was going to need his strength, all of it, before this night was over.

He found Morris in his harness-room living quarters, boards freshly nailed over the place where Reston Lane had *that morning* blown a hole through the wall in his attempt to assassinate Arlen Cooper.

That morning!

That was the thing.

This was still only Sunday night. Longarm had *not* slept through Tom Smith, Jr.'s execution by hanging. The kid was still in that jail in Denver.

And now, between what Saundra had just said and an item in that week-old *Denver Post*, there was a damned good chance that Longarm could give the Denver County sheriff the proof needed to stop that scheduled trip to the gallows.

He had to check a few things first, of course. He had to have a quick conversation with the old hostler, examine some evidence.

And—he took the Ingersoll out and checked it—he had to find some way to get to Denver tonight, as early as was humanly possible.

As weak as he was feeling and as far away as it was, he hoped to hell he did not have to get on a horse and ride south to the city.

But he would if he had to.

He stormed into Morris's room and practically rattled the old man's brains when Longarm grabbed him by the shoulder and turned him toward the wall.

"What's that?" Longarm demanded.

"What the hell? I . . ."

Longarm let go of Morris and took the few steps necessary. He bent and picked up the burlap sack. A broad smile crossed his face when he looked inside it.

"You better know what you're doing, Marshal, or they'll have your badge for this. I'm going to report it, you know. I swear I will."

"If you don't shut your mouth," Longarm said coldly, "and do what I told you, you'll have to make your report in writing. 'Cause I'm gonna reach down your throat and rip your tongue out for a necktie. I still think you're the one that tipped the crowd to where Cooper was last night. Come to think of it, Louis, I just might decide to put you in cuffs an' charge you with the obstruction of justice."

Longarm was not entirely positive of the legality of such a charge under the state statutes, questions of jurisdiction aside, but if *he* was unclear on the subject, the damned railroad agent had to be too.

Louis shut up.

"Hang that signal now, damn it."

"All right," the agent grumped. "But you just better know what you're doing."

"Let me worry about that. You just hang the signal."

Louis hauled a short stepladder out of the storage closet built into the side wall of the tiny depot and lugged it down along the tracks. He lighted a brass bullseye lantern with a red lens and climbed the ladder to hang it on the signal arm, replacing the green-lensed lantern that had been swinging there.

"You better—"

"I know what I'm doing," Longarm said impatiently.

The last southbound passenger train had already rolled through Childs Ferry on its way to Denver. The only thing left due south tonight was a special freight that was not scheduled to make any stops between Julesburg and Denver.

The red signal lantern would damn sure stop it, though, Longarm knew. Not only was it against the law for a train to roll through a red signal, it was damned well deadly to do so. And, laws aside, trainmen tended to value their own asses about as much as anybody did. The stop signal would pull them down to a brake-smoking halt no matter what their orders read.

Longarm was keyed up, bobbing up and down on the balls of his feet, despite the weakness that still tugged at his limbs.

He wanted a drink, but he had nothing with him. He knew better than to ask Louis for anything the bastard could refuse. There was no time to go over to the saloon for a quick one. The southbound was due within minutes, and he did not want to take a chance.

He could not afford that, and neither could Tom Smith, Jr.

Off to the north he heard a mournful howl as the special freight's whistle sounded. Another minute or two and he could see the bright gleam of the carbide reflector lamp rushing closer in the night.

"You better—"

"Shut up, Louis."

The standard-gauge locomotive roared south, a big son of a bitch to make the long, deceptive gain in elevation between the main line tracks and Denver.

It roared up to the jerkwater depot at Childs Ferry, and past.

"What the hell?" Longarm said.

Louis gave him a disgusted look. "You can't stop a thirty-

157

car freight like a damned horse and buggy," he said. "Listen."

Longarm did. Amid the clack and clatter of steel wheels crossing the rail joints he could hear now the high-pitched squeak of handbrakes being set against the awesome inertial progress of the moving train.

Brakemen scrambled over and between the cars, and at both the front and the rear of the freight there were men with lanterns signalling to one another.

They had seen the red lantern, and they were stopping.

"They'll be a mile down the road before they get it all shut down," Louis said.

"Will they back up to the depot?"

"Yeah." Louis made the word sound like it tasted bad in his mouth.

"Good." Longarm folded his arms and stood where he was, waiting for the train to come to him.

When it finally did he swung up the steps of the caboose to join the conductor. He already had his wallet open and his badge displayed before the local agent could open his mouth.

"Get me to Denver," he ordered. "Fast."

The conductor was no happier about the situation than Louis had been. He too was making noises about having Longarm's badge.

Longarm grinned to himself. There was only so much meat on his tail to be chewed. And if this didn't work out, why, there would likely be no badge to lose to these railroad people anyway.

Billy Vail would snatch it away before they ever got their shot at it.

Chapter 14

The conductor shook him awake as the freight was pulling into the yards at Denver. The rest had not been a long one, but it had damn sure been helpful. If he did not yet feel human again, he at least felt halfway to it. Longarm thanked the man despite the conductor's continued foul humor over the unplanned and unauthorized halt. He swung down off the freight as soon as its speed had come down to a walk.

The hackney cab stand was empty at this hour, with no passenger trains scheduled for arrival until morning. Longarm walked to the nearby and always open Harvey House. He did not regret having to make the side trip. His stomach was growling with hunger. He had left Childs Ferry before Saundra could cook those thick, juicy steaks, and the thought of them was gnawing at him now.

"Boy."

"Yes, sir?" A kid of twelve or so, who should have been at home in bed but was not, was hanging around inside the resturant.

"It's worth a quarter to me if you can find me a cab and have it here before I've time to finish one of these cardboard things they call sandwiches here."

The boy's eyes went wide. "You mean that, mister?"

"I said it, didn't I?"

"Yes, *sir*." The boy dashed out into the night and was out of sight before Longarm could reach the counter where sandwiches, coffee, and aging pastries were available around the clock.

Longarm wolfed down two of the soggy sandwiches and stuffed another into his coat pocket to eat on the way. Before he could get half of his coffee down the grinning kid was back with his palm extended and there was a hack stopped in the street beyond the Harvey House windows.

"Thanks." Longarm paid for his meal and gave the boy the entire thirty cents of pocket change he got back. The boy's eyes bugged with pleasure. Longarm smiled. He could remember the now distant times when thirty cents in cash money would have been a fortune worth a prince's ransom to him. He went out and got into the cab.

"Where to, mister?"

"I'm looking for a whorehouse," Longarm said.

"Any preference?"

"I don't know the address right off hand, but it's operated by a woman called Dora LaRue. Do you know it?"

The cabbie looked unhappy, but he nodded. "Let me give you a tip, mister. I mean, it don't make no never mind to me where you swing your pick. The truth is, see, I'll get a gratuity, so to speak, from the house, wherever I take you. So it really don't make any difference to me. But my advice to you, friend, is to pick another place. We got lots of them to choose from in the city, and if you'll trust me I'll take you to a real nice place instead. Clean girls. Never no worries about what's in your purse that you hadn't figured to leave behind. You know?"

"Dora's will do," Longarm said.

The cabbie shook his head. "I'm just trying to do you a favor, friend. Honest, I am. Doesn't matter a dime's worth to me, see. But this Dora's place has got so bad that the police raided it last week. In this town, mister, that's *bad*. Around here we believe in letting a man have his pleasures

160

or allowing him to be as much a damn fool as he wants, so—"

"Dora's place," Longarm interrupted firmly.

The driver shrugged his shoulders in resignation and took up his lines. He spoke to his team, and the horses moved off at a smart trot, their shoes clattering and sparking on the macadam pavement.

The drive was a long one, all the way up to the north edge of the city. Longarm finished his last sandwich while he rode. He felt much better with his stomach full again and his strength was returning. His back still stung slightly under the wrapping of bandages Saundra had put on him, but it was not enough to worry with.

While he rode, too, he checked the cylinder of the Colt to make sure it was fully charged. He could not remember reloading after the scrap with Reston Lane, but he must have done so. The gun carried five stubby cartridges in the cylinder, with the sixth chamber left empty to ride under the hammer. He pulled a loose round from his pocket and dropped it into the sixth chamber, then felt of his vest pocket too to make sure the little derringer was where it was supposed to be. Finally, satisfied, he closed his eyes and rested for the last few minutes of the drive.

The hackney left him off on the edge of a quiet neighborhood. A block away there were saloon lights glowing bright even though this was a Sunday night. Here on a dimly lighted stretch of side street there was mostly darkness.

"That house over there," the cabbie said, accepting his fare and a tip that was intended to show Longarm's appreciation of the man's good will. The fellow had tried to steer him right.

"Thanks."

Longarm let himself through a gate in a low fence surrounding the whorehouse and approached the front door.

The path had been paved and gravel spread over the paving stones so that his footsteps were loud. Obviously someone was stationed inside to watch and to listen, because the door swung open to greet him before he had time to knock.

"Yeah?" The person doing the greeting was a man, not the madam. He was a small fellow with bad teeth and a slight stoop to his shoulders. He did not look particularly friendly or welcoming.

Longarm took his hat off and smiled. "You're open for business, I hope."

"Yeah. C'mon in." The man—he was too small to be a bouncer—swung the door wide. But that was the extent of the welcome he gave. If a customer expected to be pampered here, someone else would have to do it.

Longarm was led into a parlor that was almost a parody of what a whorehouse is supposed to be. The whole place was done in gold and scarlet, gold brocades and scarlet velvets. Even the carpet was patterned in gold and red.

There were no other customers in sight at the moment. Two bored-looking whores were playing some version of rummy at a games table in one corner, while another was reading a magazine. All three showed their teeth to him when Longarm entered. He got the impression—but he was not absolutely positive about it—that they were smiling.

The three whores exchanged a round of glances so subtle that Longarm almost missed seeing them. In some mysterious manner they achieved an agreement this way, and one of the girls who had been playing cards laid her hand down and drifted over to his elbow.

She took his arm and smiled at him, laying her cheek briefly against his shoulder. She smelled of perfume and scented powder, and actually looked better at close range than she had from across the room. Scrape off half a pound of artificial beauty and she probably would have been quite pretty, Longarm thought.

"What can I do for you, honey?"

He smiled back at her. "Lots of things, I'd bet," he said. "But first, could a man get a drink here? I'm not in a hurry, and I have a considerable thirst."

"Sure thing, honey. But business first, okay? This is a high-class place, you understand. Ten dollars an hour buys whatever you like. That covers drinks, whatever. Nothing weird, though. You got to see Dora about anything special. And for anything real different, you might not have your pick of the girls."

"You look just fine to me," Longarm said. He handed her a double eagle, which disappeared so fast he thought she might have done better as a sleight-of-hand artist than in her chosen line of work.

"I like you, honey," she said, giving his arm a squeeze. "My name is Fanny, and if you'll tell me what you'd like to drink I'll serve you." She winked at him. "Any way you like."

"Rye whiskey," he said. "Maryland made if you have it." He smiled at the girl who called herself Fanny, but he was thinking about little Carrie Smith.

Little Carrie probably was not more than four, maybe five years younger than this Fanny. By the calendar, anyway. The two were centuries apart in all the ways that really counted. It was up to Longarm to see that Carrie Smith did not ever catch up with Fanny.

Fanny led him to a scarlet upholstered loveseat at the side of the parlor and seated him, then whisked quickly away with a provocative wiggle in her rather nicely shaped behind.

She disappeared briefly in the back of the place and

163

returned with a generously large glass of cheap rye whiskey that definitely was not what Longarm had had in mind for a drink.

He sniffed of the stuff and tasted it, but managed to keep his face expressionless. The whiskey, bad to begin with, had not been cut. Quite the contrary. Someone had added raw alcohol and probably caramel coloring to it, increasing the potency of the drink. A few knocks of the liquid fire, especially if the man had been drinking already and was not able to detect the difference, and the poor bastard would be passed out and snoring. Madam Dora and company could then pick the poor fool clean and toss him out in a handy alley, and likely he would not even remember the next day what a wonderful time he had had. Longarm sipped at his drink very slowly.

"Well, you said you weren't in a hurry, honey. Neither am I." Fanny slipped in under his arm and pressed herself against him as snug as a kitten in an afghan. Obviously she would get her cut whether the customer took her upstairs or passed out on the spot. And, in fact, she probably would prefer it for the guy to go cold here in the parlor and save her the trouble of getting out of her stays.

Longarm took another small sip of the lousy whiskey and kept his eyes open.

"Shu . . . shu't . . . *shouldn't* . . ." His mouth twisted with the effort of trying to force the word. He grinned, his face slack, with his satisfaction of achieving the goal. "Shouldn't h'of . . ."

Longarm's face went blank, and his head lolled backward. He began to breathe slowly, not quite a snore. He was passed out cold, at least to all outward appearances. He had been working on this phony drunk for the better part of an hour. It should look real enough. Fanny had no idea either of what he might have had to drink before he arrived here or of his capacity to hold his liquor.

During the time he had sat there drinking and being cosseted by the pretty whore, he had seen several other customers come and go. Twice he had caught a glimpse of the doorman.

But there had been no sign of the people he came here to see.

Since he was not sure of where he could find them, the next best thing, he reasoned, would be to bring them here to him. Hence the pretense of passing out.

He continued his slow, stertorous breathing. Fanny stayed with him for several minutes, then gently disengaged herself from under his arm to sit upright on the loveseat with a long, relieved exhalation of her breath.

"Charlotte Mae," she asked politely, "would you please ask Mr. Jones to come to the parlor for a moment?"

Someone, presumably Charlotte Mae, giggled and left the room.

She was not gone long. Her footsteps went toward the back of the house. He heard the sound of a door being opened on squeaky hinges, and then footsteps on uncarpeted wooden stairs. The front stairs to the upstairs portion of the house, where normal trade was conducted, were carpeted. It was exactly this sort of thing that had made Longarm hesitant about announcing himself to begin with. A wrong turn in the unfamiliar place, and his birds would have flown. He was glad he had waited. Besides, the whiskey, once he had gotten used to it, had not been all that bad.

Charlotte Mae returned almost at once, and there were the heavier footfalls of booted feet behind her.

Two men, Longarm thought. Only two. That was something of a disappointment, but two would be enough, if they were the right two.

He waited until the new arrivals in the parlor were standing in front of him. Then he popped his eyes open wide and let out a loud chortle.

He looked and sounded like a suddenly wide-awake drunk, but the truth was that he was getting a look at the men Charlotte Mae had brought.

He chortled again, but this time it was genuine.

Carrie Smith had described in considerable detail the three men she and her brother claimed had come to the Smith place and exchanged the stolen Diamond F horses for Tom Smith's cobs.

The girl had said they were all larger than average men, one with black, shaggy hair and a prominent nose, one dark-complected but with dirty blond hair and a hairy mole on the shelf of his jaw, the third with black hair and eyes that reminded her of a snake's.

Snake Eyes and Mole Jaw were standing in front of Longarm now. He grinned at them, still pretending to be harmlessly drunk.

"What d'you think?" Mole Jaw asked Snake Eyes.

"What the shit," Snake Eyes said. "Bop him one an' he won't remember none of it tomorra anyhow."

"I reckon." Mole Jaw pulled a sap from his hip pocket. The thing was of carefully tanned and crafted leather, a slender pouch roughly two inches in diameter and nine inches long. From the way Mole Jaw handled it, Longarm guessed that it was filled with birdshot. A whack from a thing like that could give a man a hell of a headache—if he ever woke up again.

Mole Jaw smiled at the supposed drunk in front of him and leaned closer with the sap balanced in his right hand.

His eyes went wide, though, when he found himself looking cross-eyed into the muzzle of a blued steel Colt revolver. He had to cross his eyes to see it because the cold ring of the muzzle was pressed tight against the bridge of Mole Jaw's nose.

"Howdy, boys," Longarm said pleasantly.

"Aw, shit," Snake Eyes muttered. Mole Jaw did not say anything. Longarm got the impression that Mole Jaw could not have piped out any kind of squawk just then.

"Look, mister, we . . . we wasn't going to *do* anything, you see, but see that you was okay, because the girl there, she said you'd passed out, and . . . uh . . ."

"Sure," Longarm agreed. "How about if we go downstairs and look for your friend?" he asked.

"Friend? We don't know what you mean, man. I swear we don't."

"If you say so. But we'll take a look anyway."

"Look, customers aren't allowed in the private parts of the place. You understand that, don't you, mister?"

"Sure. I understand that. But we'll take a look anyhow."

"But—"

"For God's sake, Jerry, shut up and do what the man says, will you." Mole Jaw had found his voice again.

Longarm reached out with his free hand and plucked the sap out of Mole Jaw's nerveless fingers. He tossed it aside and quickly frisked the man. Mole Jaw had a nickel-plated hideout revolver in his coat pocket. Longarm appropriated the weapon and transferred it to his own pocket, then stood and searched Snake Eyes too. Snake Eyes was carrying a spring-blade knife, a set of brass knuckles with pointed spikes on the delivery side, and a percussion derringer. Those weapons also joined Longarm's collection.

"Now," he said. "Show me the way."

"We can't . . ."

"I only need one of you to show me around," Longarm said, still in a mild, pleasant tone of voice. "I expect I could shoot one of you and ask the other to show me around the house." He smiled. "The only question is, which one do I shoot and which do I get help from."

There was no more reluctance to lend a hand when help was politely requested. In fact, both Mole Jaw and Snake Eyes seemed positively eager to be of service.

The thugs were likely making the incorrect assumption that this tall, nicely dressed customer had decided to rob the house, and Longarm saw no reason at the moment to confuse them with unnecessary facts. Better to let them go on thinking whatever they wished for another minute or two.

Mole Jaw led the way to the back of the house, with Snake Eyes close behind and anxious lest the man with the gun think he was any less cooperative than Mole Jaw.

"Here. Right down here," Mole Jaw said, pointing to a closed door.

The house, Longarm noticed, really had been a house at one time, the residential kind. The kitchen looked familiarly homey and scrubbed, with copper pots hanging attractively from a rack on the wall and a tall, ornate range next to a pie safe in the corner.

"You fellows lead the way," Longarm said. "You can say or do anything you like on the way down, but if I get upset on the way down those stairs I don't figure to be the only one to suffer for it."

"Uh, yes, sir." Snake Eyes muscled his way in front of Mole Jaw and started the parade down the steps into the cellar.

The basement was as well lighted if not so grandly furnished as the parlor above. The walls were of raw, unmortared stone and the ceiling nothing but the unfinished joists of the ground floor. A coal furnace was rusting in one corner. The remainder of the space was occupied with scatterings of cast-off chairs, a sagging couch, and a threadbare rug laid over the dirt floor.

A man fitting Carrie Smith's description of Big Nose to a tee was sitting in one of the chairs. His feet were propped up on an empty whiskey crate, and a nearly full bottle of whiskey was on the floor beside his chair. He looked like he had had much more than had so far been removed from that bottle, but there were plenty of empties set here and there in the basement that he could have been working on previously.

Big Nose blinked and came halfway to his feet when he saw his pals coming down the stairs with a stranger.

"Easy," Longarm suggested briskly, authority crackling in his voice.

Big Nose blinked some more but quit moving.

Longarm herded his catch to the bottom of the stairs and waved the men into a corner, where he could keep an eye on them.

He had Big Nose turn around and bend over while Longarm searched him. The only weapon Big Nose carried was a Barlow knife too small to be considered dangerous to anything larger than a whittling stick.

"Over here now, boys. All of you." Longarm motioned them closer, using the barrel of the Colt to do the motioning. The three thugs acted like they were in a hurry to obey.

There hadn't been a real weapon among them, Longarm reflected as he pulled his cuffs out and groped in a coat pocket for the extras he had brought along.

There was not a real weapon in the crowd, and none of them exhibited a whole hell of a lot of intelligence. Bully boys, sure, but not one of them capable of planning any halfway lucrative crime. It would take someone else to do their thinking for them. These three were just a trio of dime-a-dozen plug-uglies. They could be bought by the bucketful for a handful of silver in any large city in the world, these or ones enough like them that it would not matter which was which. Interesting, Longarm thought.

He handcuffed Mole Jaw's wrist to Snake Eyes's, Snake Eyes's wrist to Big Nose, and Big Nose's wrist to Mole Jaw's, so that they were chained in a circle facing outward, their backs to the center of the circle.

If they could run like that, Longarm figured, they were damn near entitled to get away.

He smiled at them and pulled his wallet out to show them his badge. Mole Jaw had been so scared they were being robbed by a madman that he actually looked relieved to see the identification.

"Up the stairs now, boys." Longarm urged them along with the muzzle of the Colt.

"Like this? We can't, Marshal."

"Take your time, boys. I'm not in no hurry, and neither are you." He grinned. "Not any more, you aren't."

The three prisoners grumbled. They also stumbled considerably. But eventually they figured out a way to sidle off in the general direction of the steps.

Longarm ambled behind them. He was, as he had said, in no hurry at all now. He transferred the Colt to his left hand and used the right to pull out and light a good cheroot.

Chapter 15

The parlor was empty. There was no sign any longer of the
ladies of the evening. Fanny, Charlotte Mae, and their friends
had disappeared. That was only to be expected once a gun
was shown, but still Longarm did not like it. The empty
room seemed unnaturally silent and shabby with no one in
it. Longarm drifted to the side and let the three thugs precede
him as a shield.

Two figures stepped into the doorway between the parlor
and the vestibule.

Longarm smiled. "I was beginning to think you'd closed
up for the night."

"Not fuckin' likely." The woman who spoke had red hair,
clearly from a bottle, and a rasping whiskey voice. She
wore a somewhat stained gown that might once have been
elegant but which now was only a pathetic reminder of past
glories. Her hands, wrinkled and knobby with arthritis, glit-
tered in the lamplight with many rings and baubles.

"Dora, I presume," Longarm said, using his left hand to
raise his cheroot to his mouth and take a draw on it.

Dora nodded slowly, with an air of dignity that seemed
out of place on this ugly woman.

Behind her was the small man who had let Longarm into
the place some hours earlier. He was holding himself taut
and ready. Small, Longarm thought, but much more deadly
than any of the three hired musclemen. This little one was
apt to be quick and certain, not the kind to play games with.

On the other hand, a little anger, or a lot of it, sometimes leads to errors of judgment.

Longarm pointed the glowing tip of his cigar at the little man and asked. "Your dwarf?"

The fellow was good. His face did not even color. It did, however, harden. There was a slight tensing along the lines of his jaw.

Sometimes, Longarm thought, a fellow can outsmart himself. He wondered if he had just done that with the doorman and part-time bodyguard.

"Who are you, asshole?" Dora asked.

Longarm smiled at her again. "I don't believe the ladies of the Century Club are going to invite you to tea, Dora, unless you improve your language."

"Up yours, prick. Now, who do you think you are, comin' in here and waving guns around and then tryin' to walk out with three of my employees."

"Employees," Longarm mused. "I like that. So much nicer than the other ways you could've put it. Nice of you to admit it, too. I was wondering if I'd have trouble proving that in a court of law."

The old bat's eyelids fluttered at mention of the law, and the prune wrinkles around her mouth puckered. "Are you saying you're the law, mister?"

Mister. Not asshole or prick, but mister. It was an improvement.

"Deputy United States marshal," he admitted. "Long by name."

"You work for Vail, then?" He thought she looked a touch pale.

The dwarf was standing partially obscured behind the woman, who was half a head taller than he. He went up onto his tiptoes to whisper into her ear.

"The one they call Longarm," she said grimly.

"Exactly," Longarm admitted.

"Tyrone tells me it won't do any good, but I might as well ask. What's it gonna cost me to get out of this?"

"No sale," he said. His voice was flat. His good humor at catching up with these people had vanished, and all the banter had drained out of him. Bribes angered him, no matter who they were offered to, but it was doubly bad when someone tried to buy him.

"Ty!" Her voice was soft. Before she finished speaking she was flinging herself sideways.

The little man already had his revolver in hand. Probably she thought that it would give her man enough of an edge. But Longarm was standing behind the three handcuffed thugs, and they must not have seen that he too had no need to reach for a holstered weapon.

Tyrone's gun barked, and Big Nose went down screaming with a bullet in his stomach. He fell, dragging the other two with him. Not that they were unwilling. All three were trying to dive out of the line of fire, but the handcuffs kept them more or less where they were since each was trying to jump in a different direction.

Longarm took his time. Better one straight shot than two fast noises.

He squeezed off the round when the muzzle of his Colt was directed point-blank at Tyrone's forehead, and the little man went down like a poleaxed beef. His face was virtually unblemished save for the small red dot that appeared just over the bridge of his nose. There was not much left of what had been the back of his head, however.

On the floor at Longarm's feet, Big Nose was thrashing around and still screaming. Mole Jaw and Snake Eyes had finally gotten together on a direction in which to pull and were trying to drag Big Nose with them to the safety of the nearest sofa.

Dora LaRue was standing in the vestibule, staring with disbelief at the lifeless body that had been Tyrone. She was pale and shaking, and her hands were trembling inside a furry muff that did not match her gown.

A tear squeezed out of the corner of one eye and left a trail in the powder that caked her face. "He was a good little bastard," she whispered. Her eyes flashed hate when she looked at Longarm. "You did this to him."

"Uh-huh."

"You..."

"Dora," Longarm said. "You'd best drop that muff now, or I'm just gonna have to figure you got you a little hideout gun tucked away in it. I wouldn't really like to shoot a woman, so whyn't you drop it now."

"You bastard," Dora hissed. "You gunned him down in cold blood."

Longarm's view of the situation was somewhat different, but this did not seem a good moment for rhetoric. That was best left to lawyers and courtrooms.

"You gunned poor Tyrone down," Dora ranted on, "and now you're threatening to shoot a defenseless woman. You fucking coppers are all alike, aren't you. You..."

Her hands came forward in a sweeping, theatrical gesture, the muff remaining over her right wrist.

Longarm angled the Colt up and shot her in the chest.

Her involuntary muscle contraction at the impact caused her hands to clench, and there was a sharp crack of sound from inside the muff. A spearpoint of flame licked out of the end of it, singeing the fur.

Dora's knees buckled, and she sagged face forward onto the floor. Scarlet bright enough to match the carpeting seeped over the front of her dress and flowed sluggishly down onto the bright red of the floor covering. But Dora no longer cared any more than Tyrone did.

Longarm checked the vestibule and the stairwell leading to the second floor, but there was no one else near. He could hear some wailing from the rooms upstairs and a swift scurry of bare feet moving, but there was no one around who seemed a threat.

He jammed the end of the cheroot between his teeth and went back into the parlor.

"Come out from behind there, boys. We have to go find a cab, a cop, and a doctor, in that order."

"Yes, sir." Snake Eyes and Mole Jaw crawled out from behind the sofa, dragging a mercifully unconscious Big Nose with them.

Chapter 16

Billy Vail leaned back in the swivel chair that Longarm had occupied so briefly. The marshal tapped thoughtfully on his front teeth with the end of a pencil he was holding, then leaned forward to study the papers on the surface of his desk once more.

Finally he raised his eyes enough to look at Longarm, who was sitting silent and just as thoughtful in the straight chair in front of the desk.

"It looks like you had yourself some fine weekend, Long." The fact that no nickname was used sounded ominous. Vail tapped the slim sheaf of paperwork. "One formal complaint from a railroad agent at some little town I never heard of. One formal complaint from a railroad conductor. One informal note from the chief of police and a . . . uh . . ." he leaned forward to glance at the wording handwritten in ink at the top of that sheet, "memorandum of inquiry from a county court judge. None of those folks seems all that appreciative of your efforts on behalf of your government this weekend past, Long."

The marshal reached into his pocket and pulled out a flimsy sheet of yellow paper. "Balanced against that I will say that we received a wire this morning thanking us for 'our,' and I use the word loosely, assistance in the apprehension of a certain Arlen Cooper, wanted by Weld County for the crime of murder."

"It's all in the report, Billy," Longarm said.

"You know as well as I do that Henry hasn't finished typing your report."

"I gave you the high points." Longarm squirmed a bit in his chair. The damn thing felt awfully hard and unaccommodating this morning.

"Yes. High points indeed." Vail leaned back in his chair again and gave Long a baleful look. "Where is the boy right now?" he asked.

"Young Smith? He's still over at the jail. Sleeping, the last I heard. At least that's what they're calling it. The kid passed out colder'n shit when they told him he wouldn't swing. They're letting him rest and said they'll clean him up and release him to me this afternoon. I figured to take him north on the afternoon train. If it's all right with you, that is. I have to go up there anyway to collect the gear I left in Childs Ferry and bring that rented horse back to town. But that's only if it's okay with you." He was careful to make no mention of any promises involving a certain Miss Emma Emry, although he had not forgotten them. And he probably owed some apologies and explanations to Saundra too, after running out like that.

Billy Vail grunted.

"Those notes from the local boys, Billy, why, hell, they've just got their tails twisted because I didn't call them in so they could be there at Dora's place with a bunch of megaphones and newspaper reporters. Naturally I would've brought them in on the arrest, except I didn't think there was time."

"Naturally," Billy said in a dry voice.

"Of course I would have. As for the railroad, well, there just wasn't any way to get back down here in time. I know no one, not you or the locals or George Foster, would want an innocent kid to hang."

"There are still the jurisdictional questions, Long," Billy

said. "It's one thing to step on toes when you have the right, but it is quite another when you have no business monkeying into things."

For the first time in some minutes Longarm smiled. "I know it didn't look like a federal matter, Billy. Not right out front, it didn't. But there were those letters, you know. That makes it our business, the way I see it."

"Run this by me one more time, Long."

Longarm swallowed hard. It was plain dumb-assed luck that he'd found the excuse. And that was all it was. An excuse, pure and simple. He hadn't come up with even that feeble excuse until last night.

He had never really doubted Tom Smith, Jr.'s innocence on the horse theft charges after he talked to Carrie. But what he had had to do was find the real horse thieves and prove that they, not young Tom, had done the stealing.

No one, probably not even George Foster deep down, had ever really believed that the boy had stolen those horses for profit.

No one had stolen them for profit, because they had been exchanged for fresh mounts and left in the Smith corral.

It was only reasonable to assume that whoever had taken the three animals was in a large hurry to get someplace else. That place had turned out to be Childs Ferry.

The key to it had been with the two things that happened to him on Sunday evening. He had read parts of that old Denver newspaper Saundra had had in her house. And then she had told him about the livery man worrying about losing money on three horses that had been left with him overlong.

They were the same three horses Longarm had stood right beside on Saturday morning when he was talking to Morris, the animals in the box stalls. Morris did not pamper his own stock with box-stall quarters. Those were reserved for paying customers.

Longarm had stood right there and practically leaned his elbow on one of the missing saddles that had been taken from the Diamond F along with the horses. The third saddle was Foster's fancy rig that Morris had been thoughtful enough to put into a burlap sack and keep in his own bedroom so no harm would come to it. But Longarm had not noticed at the time, because he was so preoccupied with his pursuit of that son of a bitch Cooper.

The different things fell into place, though, when he realized where the horses and the saddles were. And that the men who had really stolen George Foster's horses had gotten the hell out of Denver, fogged it to Childs Ferry, and caught a train *back* to the city.

These were not country boys or any kind of horsemen he was dealing with. They were city toughs who had had to run and then wanted to get back to the alleys where they belonged just as quick as they safely could.

"There were the two things in Monday's paper that kinda tied together if you looked at them slaunchways, Billy," Longarm explained.

"Such as?"

"The first was that robbery of the Wells Fargo courier. He was transferring money, a wire mesh reinforced sack of it chained to his wrist, when three men jumped him and knocked him out. They cut the bag off him with bolt cutters and lit out on foot toward the north. One of the brass-buttons chased after them, but they gave him the slip somewhere around Berhardt's Tavern."

"So?"

"So that was almighty close to an address given in the paper for a raid the police were making at just about that same time of night, in the wee hours of Sunday, on Dora's place."

"I still don't see how the two things tie together, Long."

"It isn't all that involved, Billy. Dora's was pretty bad about customers being robbed and dumped. That's why the police were raiding her and trying to put some manners into her people."

Vail nodded.

"And I figured that somebody who's that greedy in one line might be greedy enough to be involved in other kinds of robberies as well. Hell, we both know that men talk a lot when their drawers are on the foot of the bed. A place like Dora's would be an ideal setup to get information for robberies outside the house too."

Vail steepled his fingers and peered into them. "I can accept that, so far."

"So what I got to thinking was, what if those jaspers who took down the Wells Fargo courier were working out of Dora's? What if they hauled butt back there with the loot and got there just about in time to see a bunch of damn cops all over the place? What do you think they'd do, Billy? Me, I think they'd keep on running, but just far enough and fast enough to get out of the way. Soon as they could, they'd be heading for the hole again. Which, of course, is exactly what they done."

"Interesting," Vail said. "And, in fact, your speculations have been proven correct."

"The police found the loot?"

"The currency, no. But they did find what was left of the courier pouch. It had been cut open and stuffed behind a loose stone in the cellar wall."

Longarm grinned.

"But," Vail said, "the whole thing is strictly under the jurisdiction of the local authorities. Where do these mysterious pieces of United States mail come into the picture?"

Longarm was still smiling. "Inside that courier bag, Billy, there was some pieces of outgoing mail that the Wells Fargo man was supposed to put in the drop box after he'd made the money transfer."

Vail rolled his eyes heavenward. "Those letters hadn't been *mailed* yet, Long. They are not the responsibility of the United States government until they are dropped into an appropriate, duly authorized receptacle."

"Are you sure about that, Billy?"

"I'll have to check the regulations to be positive, but I'm reasonably sure, yes."

Longarm shook his head and grinned. "It's a good thing you know more about these things than I do, Billy. I'd have sworn that they were in our jurisdiction once somebody stamped them. Looks like I was sure wrong about that, so I reckon I only *thought* I had proper jurisdiction in this case."

Vail looked at his chief deputy and shook his head, but he was smiling a little. "I don't know what kind of dumb son of a bitch you take me for these days, Longarm, but you and I both know you hadn't any idea at all there was any mail, not so much as a *smell* of mail, involved until you read that newspaper article last night. And by then you'd been on the case for forty-eight hours."

"Billy!" Longarm managed to look wounded, hurt to the quick. He spread his palms wide in a show of great innocence.

Vail sighed. "All right, damn it. The mail angle, weak as it is, gives me a card to play when the locals start making smart remarks about my people's boots and their people's toes." He shook his head. "There are times, Longarm, when I think you are the plain old luckiest son of a bitch I have *ever* run across."

"Do you know what *I* think, Billy?"

The marshal grunted.

Longarm smiled. "I think that is gonna be one happy

little girl that I take a live brother home to this afternoon. And I expect I'd be willing to bend a bunch of rules to make a thing like that happen from time to time." He sobered. "That is, if I can have the time to take Tom home?"

Billy leaned back in his big, comfortable chair and closed his eyes. "Go. If I don't give you permission you'll probably do it anyway, so go. Get out of here. *But be here on time tomorrow morning, or else.*"

Longarm went quickly, before the boss could change his mind. He sighed as he headed out the door. It was a sad but true shame that there were no connections he could possibly make to get back to Denver tonight. Tomorrow night would be the very earliest he could hope to get back.

No point in fretting about that now, though. He could send Billy a wire from Childs Ferry explaining the problem. If nothing else, Billy could take the day off Longarm's personal time. He had, after all, worked the whole weekend through, hadn't he?

He was still marshalling his arguments along those lines as he walked out the door and down the stone steps of the federal building.

He was whistling a cheery tune as he walked.

Watch for

LONGARM AND THE INLAND PASSAGE

eighty-ninth novel in the bold
LONGARM series from Jove

coming in May!

Explore the exciting Old West with
one of the men who made it wild!

The hottest trio in Western history
is riding your way in these giant

adventures!

The Old West Will Never be the Same Again!!!

___08768-8 LONGARM AND THE LONE STAR LEGEND $3.50

___08769-6 LONGARM AND THE LONE STAR RESCUE $3.50

___08391-7 LONGARM AND THE LONE STAR DELIVERANCE $3.50

___08517-0 LONGARM AND THE LONE STAR BOUNTY $3.50

___08518-9 LONGARM AND THE LONE STAR VENGEANCE $3.50

Prices may be slightly higher in Canada.